The Forgetters

STORIES

GREG SARRIS

BERKELEY H CALIFORNIA
HEYDAY
50

"A Woman Meets an Owl, a Rattlesnake, and a Hummingbird in Santa Rosa"
was previously published, in slightly different form, in *Emergence Magazine*.

Library of Congress Cataloging-in-Publication Data
Names: Sarris, Greg, author.
Title: The forgetters / Greg Sarris.
Description: Berkeley, California : Heyday, 2024.
Identifiers: LCCN 2023034457 (print) | LCCN 2023034458 (ebook) | ISBN
9781597146302 (paperback) | ISBN 9781597146319 (epub)
Subjects: LCGFT: Short stories.
Classification: LCC PS3569.A732 F67 2024 (print) | LCC PS3569.A732
(ebook) | DDC 813/.54--dc23/eng/20230724
LC record available at https://lccn.loc.gov/2023034457
LC ebook record available at https://lccn.loc.gov/2023034458

Cover Art: Adobe Stock/abrakadabra
Cover Design: Archie Ferguson
Interior Design/Typesetting: de Vicq Design
Interior Art: Adobe Stock/abrakadabra

Published by Heyday
P.O. Box 9145, Berkeley, California 94709
(510) 549-3564
heydaybooks.com

Printed in East Peoria, Illinois, by Versa Press, Inc.

10 9 8 7 6 5 4 3 2 1

As always, in gratitude to the Mountain

Contents

Good Morning

Coyote's twin granddaughters, Answer Woman and Question Woman, landed on a fence rail high atop Sonoma Mountain to chatter away and tell stories, as they have on so many days. Sonoma Mountain has always been a special place for Coast Miwok and Southern Pomo people. It is said that Coyote was sitting atop Sonoma Mountain when he decided to create the world and people. But that is just one story. There are many stories, as the Mountain itself has so many things—rocks and animals, birds and grasses, fish, frogs, springs and creeks, trees—and each thing has a story. Some of the stories take place in a sacred time before this time, when the birds and animals were all people living on the Mountain. But regardless of the time, the stories connect with one another, just as the animals and plants and all other things on Sonoma Mountain do. This is one of the many important lessons the stories teach: that since the beginning of time all of life is one family.

The best way to hear the stories is to listen to Answer Woman and Question Woman. You can find them sitting up the mountain, near a place folks call Gravity Hill. Some people will tell you they are a pair of crows. Others will say the twin sisters are human, claiming to have seen two identical-looking women with long, dark hair leaning against the same fence rail, talking. In any event, this is their predicament: Answer Woman can tell all the stories, but she cannot think of them unless she is asked. Question Woman, on the other hand, cannot remember a single answer, not one story, and she must always ask her questions in order to hear the answer again.

One day, it was early, the sun a mere line of light above the Mountain's peak. The sisters were already squawking, bickering, which wasn't unusual, although this was especially early in the day for it.

"I don't like the stories you've been telling," said Question Woman.

"Can't you even say, 'Good morning'?" quipped her sister.

"Okay. Good morning."

"So, what's the problem, Sister Question Woman?"

"You're not telling Creation Stories, the stories from that time before this time when all the animals and birds were still people."

"Well, there are other stories that must be told: the Forgetter Stories."

Part One

The sisters sat a long while. Birds sang. The sky was clear. In the valley below the Mountain, thick fog had rolled back to the ocean. Question Woman, looking about, was unhappy.

"You keep telling stories about the Forgetters," she complained. "They are the people who left this Mountain long ago, and when they came back to this land they'd forgotten all the important stories. They didn't even remember that they came from the Mountain."

"But, Sister, nothing has changed," answered Answer Woman.

"How can you say that? The Forgetters are foolish. They go about hurting one another. They hurt the animals and plants. They forget that we are one family. They forget that this world is our home. Even the Coast Miwok and Southern Pomo people, who settled closest to this Mountain after Creation—even many of them have forgotten."

"Which is why I tell stories about the Forgetters: so we, all of us, remember. Those ancient people who lived at the time Coyote created the earth and people, they forgot. They, too, often acted foolish. That is what I mean by "nothing has changed." We need stories to remember, just as the ancient ones did. The people today, spread out in the towns and valleys, we are one family. These stories, like the old stories, mark the land so that we can know the stories and find ourselves. Just as an outcropping of rocks on the mountain reminds us of a story, so can a patch of clover alongside a freeway, or even an old house in Santa Rosa. We share the same sky, the same sun and moon."

"You made your point. I guess I'd forgotten."

"It's your nature, Sister."

"Now, don't make fun of me."

The sisters were quiet then. The morning grew warm. A cool breeze blew from the ocean that could be seen in the distance. Two clouds like doors appeared on the horizon.

"Didn't I ask you about those clouds?" Question Woman asked her sister.

"Yes, and I was reminded of a story. It's about the boy from Bodega Bay who opened the clouds. Will you listen now?"

Question Woman, looking embarrassed, nodded.

"Listen."

A Boy Opens the Clouds

This happened at Kalhutci, which was a village near the ocean, just north of Salmon Creek. Many people were living there after the white people came, and there weren't many places for Indians to live, only steep and barren hillsides, or rocky plateaus above the sea, like Kalhutci. Many of the people had come from the missions or from former nations and villages where it was warmer. They had gathered there sometime in the late 1860s, when there was work for them on nearby ranches and farms. The cold, salty air caused them to shiver night and day. "You can't build a fire big enough to keep us warm," they complained to the few Native coastal villagers. But even these villagers suffered the cold at Kalhutci, and they acknowledged how difficult it could be. Before the white people arrived, their villages were strategically located to protect them from the wind and cold fog. Now Kalhutci—in the past no more than a summer camp—was the only plot of land a white man didn't want to own. Nothing would grow there, and the sea cliff was steep, making it difficult for the villagers to reach the only strip of beach where they were free to dig clams and pick seaweed. They worked long hours for the white man. How else could they live?

"What is this place?" people asked themselves. "Where are we?"

There was one small boy, maybe five or six years old, who, they say, had been a rascal in the cradle on his mother's back. He'd cry and screech loud enough to scare the salmon from the banks where people fished. Once, as a baby, while his mother was gathering blackberries in the hills above the bay, he drew the attention of a bear, one of the last of the grizzlies people remembered. She'd hung his cradle on a branch not five feet from where she was filling her basket with ripe fruit, and he wailed so loud it is said his cries echoed in the hills. Some villagers speculated that the grizzly wasn't a bear at all but a human, as the animal did nothing but stand on its hind feet and walk away just like that, standing upright. Those Indians from the missions argued that those old-time things didn't happen anymore, that people no longer turned themselves into bears. Whatever the case, the woman placed the cradle on her back and hurried off, leaving her basket of berries on the ground as an offering should the bear return.

One day, when the boy was only four, he said to his mother, "Why did you leave me hanging on a branch where a bear could have eaten me?"

"I was right there where I could see you," she answered. "You cried so loud the bear heard you."

Perplexed by the boy's unusual memory, his mother sought the advice of an old Indian doctor, who provided no advice but to watch the boy, saying that he had eyes that could see things other people couldn't see. Which is why, not a year later, when he began gazing at the ocean with unbroken focus, hardly ever moving or responding to anyone's words, they let him sit all day long, right there on the same rock. He didn't have to husk acorns or haul water, chores expected of other children. The villagers remembered what the old Indian doctor had told his mother: he could see things.

Some people said he was a lazy boy, spoiled, and that he saw nothing, that he'd only fooled his mother and others to get out of work. On long, cold nights and on days when the damp coastal fog hid the hills and trees, when the villagers could hardly see a foot in front of them, they continued to speculate about the boy. One woman, a friend of the boy's mother who'd been the mistress of a white fisherman from Bodega Bay, thought that the boy could see whales far out at sea, even through the dense fog. Another woman suggested, "He might be able to see when sea bass approach the waters where we fish on the beach that isn't owned by a rancher or the mill boss." The doubters from the missions agreed with the villagers who thought the boy was lazy, if not also clever because he got his mother and others to believe he had a special power. After all, the boy, when asked what he saw, never answered. When people inquired of the old Indian doctor, he too would give no answer. He told them that he was not from this place, reminding them that he, like so many others, had been taken into a mission as a young boy, and now, even farther from his home in San Jose, he doubted that in his great age he would have the chance to find his way back.

Fog settled over the land so thick people could no longer tell day from night. People could not travel about. The villagers huddled near fires, burned driftwood to keep warm. Those men

working for the ranchers, and the women who washed clothes
and kept houses, could not see their way back to Kalhutci; they
huddled at night in horse stalls to keep warm. Then the fog lifted,
and where the boy was looking there were two clouds, like doors
in the blue horizon.

Someone remembered then that it was said the wind came
from two doors in the sky. Still, the boy said nothing. But not
long after, he began huffing and puffing, blowing his breath toward the clouds. And what breath he had! "His crying as a baby
opened his lungs," his mother said. It was as if he were practicing,
getting stronger and stronger, until one cloud seemed to roll open
in the sky, and wind blew over the water to the village.

The cloud looked as if it were slightly ajar, and the wind blew
to the south. When the second cloud door opened, again slightly
ajar, the wind blew north. When both clouds opened toward the
village, the wind blew directly onto the land, east, and when they
opened in the opposite direction, the wind came back, west over
the hills, as if it were returning to the far sea from whence it came.
The boy, huffing and puffing, blew and blew, day and night. No
one doubted anymore what the boy had been seeing through the
fog. He had seen the cloud doors from where the wind comes.

Days and nights passed, and the boy didn't stop. The sky
cleared. It was so clear that the villagers could see for miles up
and down the coast. They saw whales spouting far out at sea. East
in the hills, they saw the great, tall redwoods the mill workers
hadn't found. And when more and more people came to see the
boy working his magic to open and close the clouds, the villagers

saw how many big and beautiful rocks covered the hillside above the village, for that is where the spectators gathered, sitting on the rocks to have a perfect view of the clouds opening and closing with the shifting winds.

For the most part, the villagers were happy. They could see their way down the steep cliff to dig clams and pick seaweed. Kalhutci became famous. Indians far and near journeyed to the village to see the boy who could open the clouds. The visitors brought food and offerings of clothes and blankets for the villagers. They told stories, and everyone seemed to remember that they had known about the cloud doors, or at least having been told about them. "At last, we know where to see these clouds, where the wind comes from," the visitors said. The few villagers with ancestral ties to the coast were equally surprised. "How come we didn't know before that the clouds could be seen in plain sight right where we lived?" they wondered.

But before long, people began to miss the fog. While the sun shone brightly, the wind was still very cold, more biting than the fog. People noticed how dry everything had become. Dust blew up constantly, and it was impossible to keep a good fire, for smoke blew every which way as the villagers and their guests huddled to keep warm.

"Maybe just once a week, on Sundays, when the ranchers and mill bosses give us time off, open the clouds. Just on Sundays," the boy's mother pleaded with her son.

But he would not listen. He laughed in his mother's face and then only huffed and puffed harder. A villager, a young man insulted by the boy's disrespect for his mother, told her she should have let the bear eat him. "He's a demon," the young man said. Others weren't so harsh, but everyone agreed the boy should stop his antics.

The ranchers had been concerned for a long while about the wind. Dust blinded their cattle and horses; wind whipped the pears and apples from their trees. Of course, they would never have believed what was happening at Kalhutci. What concerned them was so many Indians gathered in one place. Their Indian herders and housekeepers had been careful to complete their chores before escaping quietly to the village, but now so many Indians gathered at Kalhutci that the sky was bright at night with firelight. When the ranchers came armed with guns, suspecting an Indian uprising, everything changed. "If you are not planning an uprising, then you are surely going to set the land on fire with all of this wind," the ranchers said before leaving on their horses.

The villagers were frightened that the ranchers would return and force them to leave the one place they could still call home. They discouraged visitors, who nonetheless continued to gather on the hillside to witness the clouds opening and closing, many of them first-time visitors, as word of the boy's power continued to travel.

"The boy must be stopped altogether," the village leaders said. But the poor mother could not stop her errant son. Even the old Indian doctor from San Jose could find no herbs to put the boy in order. "All I can do," he told the mother, "is put him to sleep for a while. I have a song for that. Maybe you can do something with him then."

This Indian doctor taught her the song. He told her not only must she sing the song one time, but she must remember it for later.

That night, alone with her son, the woman sang the old man's song, and indeed the boy fell asleep, right there on the rock where he'd been huffing and puffing, and the wind stopped. But the mother was not at peace. She knew the boy would wake with the first light of day. She knew he would immediately begin opening and closing the clouds again and that she could not possibly continue singing forever. She would have to take the boy where he could not see the clouds. And before morning she left, packing the now large child on her back to a camp deep in a hollow near Freestone, where her sister lived. And there, it is said, she stayed, and she remembered the old Indian doctor's advice, for whenever the boy threatened to run away, most likely to the ocean, she knew how to put him to sleep.

The fog returned, but it was not as it had been before the boy started his show of power. Many people claimed the boy had made the fog so dense and long lasting only so that he could have fun causing so much trouble. Soon there wasn't a visitor left on the rocks above the village. And the day would come when even the last of the villagers were gone, scattered to find other places to live after a rancher bought the last of the land there. But to this day the old timers, passing now on Highway One, might see the rocks situated like people on the hillside, or they might even see two clouds on the horizon, and remember that they are passing Kalhutci, now in stories a great village. Some claim to have seen the clouds open and close. But no one tries to huff and puff at the clouds. Let the wind be, they say.

What happened to the boy is anyone's guess. He must've learned not to tamper with the wind, for if, as a man, he came to the ocean and remembered what he had done, he never talked about it but instead went about his business and listened as people told stories about a boy who opened the clouds.

Part Two

"I had a question about Kalhutci," Question Woman said, "but I forgot it."

Answer Woman chuckled. "I also forget things. Stories, if they are good, make you ask questions. How else do we discover another story but with an answer to a question? I told you about the boy who opened the clouds, if that helps."

"Well, that's not what I was thinking, but I have another question. I mean, the stories are about the Forgetters, right? How can a boy be a Forgetter when he has no knowledge yet of the stories we must remember?"

"Very good question, Sister Question Woman. Think of it this way: Just as the boy has learned a lesson from his bad behavior, so the Forgetters must learn from what they have forgotten in their own lives. Both the boy and the adults go about without the stories. The result will often be the same, won't it? Whether they didn't know the stories or they forgot them?"

"Okay. That reminds me of what I was thinking about to begin with."

"What is it?"

"Don't rush me. I'll forget again."

"Sorry. We don't want to end up with two Answer Women. Then we will have no questions, ha!"

"Very funny."

"Okay. Sorry again. What were you thinking?"

"These stories are about the Forgetters. But it seems the Indian people still remember a lot of the stories, maybe because they didn't wander as far away after Coyote created people on top of this Mountain. My question is about the white people in the story. They didn't even know it was a boy who made the wind. How can white people, or anyone for that matter, know any stories if they have also been gone from the Mountain so long?"

"Sister, people are no different, no matter where they have been, no matter how far they have wandered or how long it has taken them to return. Stories have always happened, and they keep happening. We are connected to one another and to all of Creation wherever we are, and the stories serve as reminders. White people are a part of the land. They have returned to the place of Creation, so they must figure in the stories too. Take the story of the stranger near Nicasio. There is a road . . ."

"A stranger near Nicasio?"

"Will you let me tell the story before I forget?"

"Sorry. I'm listening."

Dissenters Find a Stranger
in Their Camp

There is a road from Nicasio to Tomales Bay. It snakes between hills where outcroppings of rocks stand like sentinels keeping watch on passersby below. The road, like many roads and even highways in this land, was once a trail used by the Natives, and when the sheriff and his posse chased the Coast Miwok off their rancheria in Nicasio, the Indians hurried along the trail to safety at Tomales Bay. But it is told that a small group veered from the path and set up camp well hidden below one of the large rocks. To this day, old timers will point to a rock and ask, "Was it that one?"

There were five people altogether, two couples and a single woman of middle age. They were frightened, and of course angry. The Spanish padres had left the rancheria to the Indians, nearly four hundred acres, after the Mexicans took over the land. The Indians then worked for the Mexicans, but it wasn't until after California became a state that the Indians were forced to leave the rancheria. Officials, apparently sent by the local sheriff, gave the Indian leaders whiskey and duped them into signing away the land. No one knows if the five individuals who left the group did so because they had lost faith in the leaders or if they might have been themselves the outcast leaders. Maybe they just didn't want to be exiled to Tomales, where it was cold and windy. They kept hidden, only burning fires at night. They hunted and gathered acorns and berries, always covering their trails. For nearly six months they lived undiscovered, until one morning they woke to find a white man next to their fire. Had he seen smoke? Certainly there was nothing left of the night's fire but embers. Who was he and where did he come from?

He sat cross-legged. Next to him was a large cloth sack that lay on the ground like the shrunken skin of a dead animal. The Indians were too stunned to think that maybe they at last had been caught. They didn't know what to do. The stranger just sat looking from the five of them to their huts, or kotchas, and then back to the ashes, which is why, after some time, one of the men approached and asked in Spanish who he was. The stranger did not answer but only looked up confused for a moment, and then he went back to looking around the small camp.

The single woman of middle age said, "Can't you see he's not Spanish or Mexican?"

"Then speak English to him," the others suggested.

She had worked for an American settler family near Nicasio, and they called her Mary, which is how she introduced herself to the white man before asking him in English what his name was. He said nothing for the longest time but then said, "I got lost in these hills," before looking away from Mary again to his surroundings.

The two Indian men were brothers, one older and taller, the second shorter and stout. Their wives, too, were sisters, though the older and taller of the two was married to the stout brother, while the shorter, younger sister had married the older brother, who, as leader of this small group, had spoken first to the white man.

The stranger didn't speak another word but continued to study the camp and surrounding hills, as if trying to get his bearings. Mary again asked the man his name. She tried Spanish, though, as was clear by his boots and overcoat and his fair skin and blue eyes, he was American. She turned then to the tall leader, whom she addressed as hoipu, or chief.

"All we know is that he is lost," she said.

"Can we believe it?" he asked Mary.

She explained that she didn't know enough English to further question the stranger. They wondered if he might be Russian, long lost after Russia had abandoned Fort Ross, farther up the coast. And yet he spoke English and he wore clothes the recent American settlers wore.

After two days, when he hadn't left the fire except for the necessary trip to the bushes, the Indians couldn't think but to believe him. They fed him acorn mush, laughing to themselves when he turned down his mouth at the taste. Roasted rabbits and quail he relished. They brought him water from a nearby creek, which he drank heartily from their watertight baskets. More than once, Mary attempted with hand gestures and her limited English to point him toward San Rafael, from whence they figured he might have wandered. She knew better than to lead him from the small encampment lest he find his way back with the sheriff. But, as it turned out, he showed little interest in leaving, only sitting by the fire while the Indians brought him food and water.

Twice a day Mary asked him his name, once in the morning when she brought him warm acorn mush and water, then again at night after a meal of meat and fresh berries while he sat watching the two brothers take turns stoking the fire. The two men and their wives worried that this stranger might take an interest in Mary and want to kidnap her. Or maybe just to have a woman friend in the camp, now that he had food and water and a fire to keep him warm at night. What else did he need?

Mary—they say her Indian name was Hatsumat—was single; she'd long been a widow, since, more than twenty years before, her husband, a Mission Indian from Sonoma, was trampled after falling from one of General Vallejo's horses. She was well into her forties, still youthful and attractive, and she'd artfully dodged the advances of men over the years, Indian or settler, but the stranger in the weeks and months ahead never made the slightest inappropriate gesture toward her; he showed no interest. So, what did this man want? It was Mary who laughed. "'What does this man want?' Look, he wants nothing. We feed him, take care of him, and all he has to do is sit there by the fire."

As if the stranger had understood the Coast Miwok language they were speaking, he was on his feet first thing the next morning, standing by the fire. "I want to help. Teach me," he told Mary.

And that's what happened. He became suddenly so industrious that the tables had completely turned, so much so that the Indians found themselves taking his place by the fire.

He learned from the older brother to make a sharp arrowhead by chipping obsidian, and from the younger brother he learned to hunt with a bow and arrow and where to find deer close to camp and how to trap rabbits and quail in the brush. The older sister taught him to stitch clothes with only a bone awl. The younger sister taught him to weave baskets, using the same awl. Soon he could make both twined and coiled baskets. And Mary taught him songs for luck in hunting, and songs, too, for crafting arrows and for focus while weaving baskets and stitching clothes. He learned that even an arrowhead and awl needed a song if the hunter and basket maker were to be successful. Soon he was doing everything. He hunted. He cooked. He hauled water from the creek, serving the brothers and their sister wives and Mary, who now all sat day and night by the fire. They didn't live in their kotchas anymore. Their abandoned kotchas soon fell apart. This stranger with no place by the fire at night found fresh willows and tule and constructed for himself a kotcha twice the size of any that had been in the camp.

He didn't visit with anyone, always retreated at night to his kotcha. They still didn't know his name. When he rested, after packing a large deer back to camp or hauling water up the hill from the creek, he sometimes sat looking at the large rock near the top of the hill. They worried that he might be attempting to gauge his whereabouts so that he could find his way from their hiding place. After all, if he found his way back to wherever he had come from, he could return with the sheriff. But he never did leave.

Soon, though, with nothing to do, this group of dissenters began to argue, not just about this stranger and whether or not he wanted to leave, or even about what his motives might be, but also about petty issues between themselves. Jealousies and suspicions arose between the brothers. When the older brother remarked that his wife, who was short and stout, would appear to others to be the wife of his short and stout younger brother, the younger brother immediately assumed the older brother desired his taller wife. The younger brother then questioned why his older brother should be deemed hoipu of the group when in fact the younger brother, though short and stout, was more agile, by far the better hunter.

The sisters, too, bickered, recalling past offenses, real or not, from their childhoods. "You stole your basket designs from me," the older and taller sister claimed. "Yes, and wasn't I the one who taught you to weave in the first place?" the younger, stouter sister retorted. Both couples suspected Mary had used a love song on the stranger, that even as she had plenty to eat and was warm enough at night, she had intentions to move into the large kotcha with the stranger. Mary found out what they were saying about her. "You fools!" she shouted. "You insult me. I loved one man and one man only, and he died under the general's horse. If I could sing any song, it would be to put each and every one of you six feet under. But I'm not that kind of person. I would sing only to shut you up, each one of you."

They knew what they needed to do. They needed to get busy again, return to the task of feeding and caring for themselves. But, alas, they discovered they could do nothing. The older brother could no longer chip obsidian to make sharp arrows. The younger could no longer hunt, much less remember where he might find rabbits or quail. Neither sister could stitch clothes or weave baskets, for they couldn't even remember how to hold an awl. Mary forgot the songs. No one remembered how to build a kotcha so that they might cover themselves at night instead of sitting by the fire, exposed to the elements in the dark.

"We've let this man do everything, and now we've forgotten," the older brother said, noting the obvious, before adding what no one wanted to hear: "We will now have to join the others in exile at Tomales Bay."

Very quickly his short, stout wife added, "We can't do that, for he'll follow us and maybe cause more trouble there."

"And think how we will look to the others, not able even to stitch a piece of clothing after this white man took everything we know," added her tall older sister.

"So, we are trapped," her short husband, the younger brother, chimed in. "We can't lead him to the trail lest he find his way to San Rafael and return with the sheriff."

Mary spoke up then. "We have no choice but to join the others at Tomales Bay without him. We must escape while he is out hunting. Who knows what he might do with us now that we've been rendered helpless?"

"How can we escape?" the older brother asked. "He never goes far enough from the camp for us to make a safe getaway. At night he sleeps with his head near the kotcha door, where he can keep an eye on us."

"We must kill him," said the younger brother.

They devised a plan whereby the older brother would place a rock on the path to the creek, causing the stranger to fall when he went for water the next morning. Once he was on the ground, the younger brother could then crush his head. They all agreed. What else was there to do?

While the others slept that night, Mary slipped away from camp. She found the trail that led to Tomales Bay, and while the morning star still shone in the sky, she returned with an old medicine woman. The old woman summoned the two brothers and their wives a short distance from the camp, out of earshot from the sleeping stranger.

"You got lazy," she told them. "You got forgetful." She looked at Mary. "You gave the stranger our songs. We do everything with songs. These old rocks on the hills—like the one here just above your camp—they contain the memory of all things and the songs. This white man has the songs, which is why you see him looking at the old rock on the hill. The rock is attracting him."

"Might he learn more from the rock?" a remorseful Mary asked. "How will we get our songs back?"

"How will we ever know how to take care of ourselves again?" the older brother asked.

"I will sing this old rock's song so that it will return the songs you need to be able to hunt and gather berries again and sew and weave baskets."

And thus, the old woman sang:

Eyes old as stars
Eyes old as stars
Eyes old as stars
My eyes old as stars

Morning dawned on the camp. The first thing they saw was the stranger's cloth sack, swollen and propped against his little kotcha.

"That's where he's keeping our songs!" Mary exclaimed.

"And our arrowheads and quail traps," said the two brothers.

"And our willow reeds and sedge roots and awls," said the sisters.

They rushed and opened the sack. Songs flew up into the air and landed in their hearts and in the trees and everywhere in the morning sky. When they emptied the sack, turning it upside down, out spilled beautiful obsidian arrowheads and awls and watertight baskets, even white man's flour and sacks of spices and herbs and seeds from faraway countries, all of which the men and women quickly gathered.

They were so busy they had not noticed that the stranger had awakened and now was but five feet away, seeing his empty sack on the ground. When they saw him, they were alarmed, frightened, until they realized that the man was just as he had been when he had first appeared, and once again he only said, "I got lost in these hills."

The old medicine woman pointed to a satchel of sweet pea seeds and instructed Mary to give the satchel to the stranger.

"Take those seeds," the old woman said, speaking to the man in English. "Put each one down as you go on your path, and that way you will not get lost."

When she asked that they return the flour and spices and herbs to the man, he refused the offer, gesturing for the small group of dissenters to keep them.

After that, they led him to the trail and pointed him to San Rafael. They went in the opposite direction, to Tomales Bay, where they joined the others who'd left Nicasio. Whatever differences the five individuals had once had with the others, whatever the reasons for veering from the group, were long forgotten. And they soon forgot below which rock the dissenters had made their camp. But they never forgot the stranger. They figured he'd let them keep his flour and spices because he was thankful for the old medicine woman's advice, and they wondered if he himself might've been escaping the sheriff. For, as it turned out, he didn't go to San Rafael but instead west and north into Sonoma County, where each spring they see clusters of beautiful pink sweet pea blossoms on trails and along roads and highways, wherever the stranger had traveled.

Part Three

"You know, sister," Question Woman said after hearing the story, "people get tricked into forgetting what they should remember."

"They let themselves get tricked," answered Answer Woman.

"Yes, like the dissenters in the story, they let themselves get too comfortable. But think about it: People, it seems, are always getting tricked, or, as you say, letting themselves get tricked. Are humans that stupid? Is that their nature once they leave this Mountain?"

"Sister," answered Answer Woman, "yes, humans forget. But have you forgotten the stories? In order to survive, the deer has legs that help her run. Birds have wings. Humans without stories are like deer without legs, birds without wings. They won't survive. That would be stupid."

"To answer your question: I am Question Woman, and I do forget the stories. Maybe I'm more human than you."

"Well, I can't remember the stories unless you ask me. We need each other the way people need stories."

"I get it."

"Speaking of birds and people, I'm reminded of a story."

"What?"

"A story. I'm reminded of a story."

"My head is so full of thinking of how people keep forgetting that *I* can't think anymore," complained Question Woman.

"All the more reason to hear the story. Will you listen?"

"What is it, Sister, what's the story? Hurry before you forget and we end up having this conversation all over again."

"It's about a man who follows an osprey."

"I'm listening."

A Man Follows an Osprey

He was a small man, thin. But his arms were incredibly long and bent at the elbows, like the angle of a bird's wings, as if at any moment he might lift into the air and follow the course of the river, just as the osprey in the sky above him. It was sometime after the Second World War. Today no one can tell you who the man was or which rancheria he came from. Even fifty years later, after the vineyards had been converted to prune and apple orchards and then back to vineyards again, even then people had forgotten, so much so that each fall when they came to cut grapes and found an old woman where the man once stood watching the soaring silver bird, they wouldn't stop to think that she might be his wife.

His arms twisted and shook, but people paid little attention. He was a nervous man and perhaps they figured his flapping arms were just another of his tics, like his uncontrollable blinking or the way he bit his bottom lip, as if otherwise it might have gotten away from him. No one considered that even as he stood watching the bird that he might want to fly. This was at Digger Bend, a wide swath of sandy beach on the Russian River below the town of Healdsburg. Many Indians were camped there during the harvest season, Pomo and Coast Miwok from different rancherias, those small, out-of-the-way, and mostly useless plots of land the U.S. government set aside early in the twentieth century for the survivors of the horrendous century before. Digger—it was a nasty word the white people used for Indians, and maybe that's how the camp got its name: from the farmers finding the Indians who harvested their crops camped there. The Indians, uncomfortable but long familiar with the white man's derision, no doubt had their own word to describe the river's bend.

A week had gone by before someone made mention of the man's peculiar behavior.

"What's he doing alongside that rock looking at the empty sky?" a large man with a handlebar mustache asked.

The men, seated in circles in the sand, looked up from their card games, and the women, once they secured their beans and tortillas from the fires, looked too.

It was twilight. The man was standing alongside a rock, its flat top waist high, and against the reddened sky his silhouette was as still as the rock, save the fluttering motion of his arms, which no doubt was what had caught the mustached man's attention.

"What's he doing?" the onlookers whispered among themselves.

"Maybe he wants to swim," a woman offered.

"How can that be? He's looking at the sky," retorted the woman next to her.

"He's seeing something," one of the men suggested. "Maybe a vision."

The mustached man, seated across the fire and laying his

winning hand on the ground for his friends to see, said, "The real question is, What's wrong with him?"

No one noticed when the thin man sat down to eat. Everyone had finished eating, and the men were again focused on their card games. The women, seated in circles, played too, though they were having more fun gossiping and laughing over stories they told. After that first time, it happened again and again: the man stood looking up at the sky and then, unnoticed, rejoined the others. Nothing changed until the fourth night, when the mustached man caught sight of an osprey above the river and saw the man's head pivoting, following the bird as it made its way downriver.

"Ah, that's it, you think you're going to be a bird," taunted the mustached man.

The thin man did not answer, even after he sat down. The mustached man felt the silent laughter thick as fire smoke in the camp. The other men were inclined to take the side of the mustached man, who had returned from the war with many decorations and now boasted a new car and a house in town. He was the envy of other men, whose wives held up these successes to them as they might hold up a fancy blanket.

"Do you know they are all laughing at you?" the thin man's wife asked when they were alone that night. "What are you doing?"

She was small and nervous, like her husband, but even more, she was self-conscious, and as much as she didn't need the attention of others, she especially didn't want their ridicule.

"I feel drawn to that bird," he answered.

"What for?"

"I feel it wants to show me something."

The next night after work, the mustached man passed around a bottle of whiskey, which emboldened him, and his friends as well, to deride the thin man, who refused the bottle when he joined the others after watching the osprey again.

"Oh, are you some kind of bird shaman?" the mustached man cracked.

A couple of the men (and not too few women) bristled at the big man's comment, still having in their minds stories of retribution from offended shamans, which the thin man might be, but then, without mentioning their thoughts, they rationalized away such stories as things of the past. After all, these were modern times and people didn't think about those things.

"I'm attracted to the bird," the thin man said, giving the mustached man and the others the same answer he had given his wife.

"Ha! Maybe he thinks the bird will help him beat me in a card game. It'll no more help him win a single hand than it'll help him find the lost box of gold."

Later that night, alone with his wife, the thin man, who had barely been able to contain himself earlier, burst out: "That's it. That's it."

"What are you talking about?" his wife asked, then whispered, "And be quiet or you'll wake the camp."

"The box of gold!" he exclaimed.

"Shhh. What about the box of gold?"

For years, stories circulated among the Indians of hidden treasures left behind by the settlers. A precious diamond a Spanish soldier had stolen off a ship and hidden in the hills above Tomales Bay. A cache of Mexican bills General Vallejo stashed in a cave near Sonoma. But none was more popular than the tale of a wooden box full of gold hidden along the Russian River by a Russian sea otter hunter who found himself unlucky enough to have to abandon his fortune when his commander at Fort Ross decided on the spur of the moment that the entire company would be returning to Russia.

"The osprey will show me where the box of gold is," he answered. "That's what I know the osprey is for. The fat fool who makes fun of me didn't know he gave me the answer. He'll see. You and I will have a new car and house."

Seeing his wife's disbelief, he further explained: "I will follow the osprey where it goes downriver each night." He raised his arms and began lifting and dropping his elbows in the motion of flying. "I have finally understood the reason the Creator has given me these incredibly long arms."

"What?" his wife scoffed. "Are you going to fly?"

"No, I will walk, or run if I have to, to follow the osprey."

"Well then, what is this flapping of your arms?"

"It's a sign. It's the final sign that I will at last have luck. The osprey, the mustached man's mention of gold . . . and now that my long arms make sense, all of these things foretell my luck."

Immediately, his wife reminded him of the other times he had discovered something that was supposedly a sign of luck: the

green stone that indicated a pool of water along the river where
he would catch a hundred salmon at least; the tiny acorn shaped
like an ace of spades that foretold luck at cards; the pieces of
a crushed old abalone shell at the mouth of the river that would
lead him at low tide to a rock laden with abalone a foot wide
or more.

"And look what happened," she said. "You come back from
the pool of water with one small catfish I can't cook. You win ten
cents playing cards, then lose enough money that I have to sell the
only pretty necklace I had. And the abalone shells, ha! You nearly
drowned looking for a rock never to be found."

She then pointed to a gunnysack stuffed with their belongings. "You know I keep your lucky charms in a cigar box to remind you of your foolery. Must I retrieve that box now and open
it for you?"

He shook his head, saying, "I want to follow the osprey for
you and me. Everyone will see—especially that fat fool—that I'm
a good husband."

"I know," she answered. Then, without a hint of anger or derision, she told him, "Go to sleep and then go to work. That's what
you can do for me."

But he did not listen. No sooner did the soaring silver bird
appear the next evening than he was cutting through the brush,
trailing it downriver.

On and on he went, until he saw against the darkened sky
the silhouette of the bird perched on a bare bay laurel branch. He
discovered then that he was alongside the pool of water where
he thought he'd catch a hundred salmon at least. Ah, that's it,

he'd thought, the box of gold is under the water. That tiny green stone wasn't meant to show me a hundred salmon but instead where the box of gold is hidden. And with that he jumped into the water. Again and again, up he came for air and down he went searching the bottom of the river with his hands, and in no time the night was completely dark and he could see nothing. But he kept searching, so convinced was he that beneath the pool of water he'd find the box of gold. When at last he emerged, cold and drenched, he saw that all he had for his efforts was a pair of bloody palms from digging in the mucky river bottom. And the osprey was no longer in the tree.

"What in the world?" said his wife, waking in the middle of the night to find her husband wet and cold, his face covered with scratches. "And look at your hands!" she cried, forgetting her own admonition to keep quiet at night in the camp.

She washed his face and wrapped his hands with strips of cloth from one of her dresses, all the while wondering—but not wanting to ask, lest she appear insensitive—how he was going to be able to work come daylight. And indeed, she had need to worry. Before noon, his blistered hands could not hold a pair of shears to cut grapes.

But he did not listen.

"No," she said when, bandaged hands and all, he saw the osprey that evening and turned to follow it.

But on he went, downriver, until he found the osprey perched atop an oak tree.

My goodness, he thought, under this very tree is where I found the acorn that would bring me luck in cards. And with that he reached into a knothole in the tree's enormous trunk, only to find that he couldn't feel to the bottom of the knothole. What a perfect place to hide the box of gold, he told himself. He found a sharp rock and began chipping away at the tree. On and on he worked until at last he felt a line of wood bent at right angles, and so excited did he become thinking he'd found the box of gold that he stuck his head into the tree, only to see clear enough, even in the dark cavity of the knothole, that what he was feeling was no more than the rough edges of the tree's inner bark. But then he couldn't get his head out. His head was stuck. Like a bull caught in a stanchion, he frantically twisted his head back and forth, as if he might unscrew himself from the tree. He pushed his shoulders into the hard trunk, then pulled back violently, all the while both kicking and bracing himself against the trunk. He was half-asleep and blue-faced when at last he found himself on the ground flat on his back. The first light of day shone pink in the sky, and he could see the myriad branches of the large oak. The osprey was not there.

He returned to camp just as the others finished breakfast before work. His head was bloodied, and it looked as if one of his ears was sliced in half. His clothes were soaked in blood.

"What did you do, follow that bird to the ends of the earth?" one of the men joked.

"What'd you do, fall out of a tree, thinking you could fly?" another man cracked.

They'd watched him run after the osprey the night before, and the night before that, two nights now, and the poor thin man appeared to have lost his mind. He looked completely dumb-founded as he stood blinking his blood-caked eyes and biting his lip.

"That bird will no more help him beat me in a card game than it will help him find that lost box of gold," the mustached man said. But even as he mocked the thin man, now there was pity in his voice.

"The osprey will help me find the box of gold," the thin man shot back. "You'll see. All of you will see."

The others continued to laugh, even if, like the mustached man, they felt sorry for the ragged and bloodied figure before them. More so, they felt for his humiliated wife, who soon enough grabbed her babbling husband by the arm and led him to their campsite, where she washed and then bandaged his wounds, using so many strips of cloth from one of her dresses that if she wore the dress it would hardly cover her legs.

"Look at you," she said. "You've lost your mind and embar-rassed me."

But even as she chastised him, he was more determined than ever.

"Look," he said to his wife, "that fat mustached man again mentioned the box of gold."

"That means nothing—nothing more than that he happened to mention it."

"Why, then, does that osprey keep showing itself to me?"

"Ospreys fly up and down the river. That's what they do."

But her poor husband, not listening, fell asleep. She watched over him as he slept soundly, only to then see him wake and once again make his way to the waist-high rock to wait for the osprey. The others had returned from work by this time, the men already in circles starting their card games, the women cooking and chatting among themselves about a couple of handsome brothers who'd been in the vineyard that day.

"Please," the thin man's wife pleaded. "You can't work in your condition, and I can't work because I have to look after you. We will starve."

She was loud, so desperate, the others had stopped their card games and chatter and were now watching.

"I know what the problem is," her husband answered. "I just have to pay attention longer. The bird was only nesting in the trees. I must keep following it until it flies off no more, until it stops for good. That's where the box of gold will be."

She began to argue once again, but no sooner had she begun to speak than the osprey was in the reddened sky and her husband was turned downriver, where in no time he disappeared past the brush.

On and on he went until, unbelievably, he found himself at the mouth of the Russian River. The ocean was endless before him. How did I get here so fast in my condition? he wondered. It must be that I'm going to find the box of gold. The osprey was in the sky. Below the fading pink horizon, he saw the rock that he'd once believed was covered with abalones a foot wide or more. It was a good distance from the shore. White-capped waves crashed against its broad base, like a beacon flashing. There, he said to himself. Why else did I not see that rock before? The box of gold must surely be under it, and here I'd been only thinking about abalones. With that, he dove into the ocean.

He swam toward the rock, marveling at how the terribly cold water carried him faster and faster, until he was but five feet from the rock's mossy, hard surface, which is when he realized that he could not stop himself, that the ebb tide had been carrying him inexorably headfirst into the rock. When a group of fishermen found him the next day, washed ashore several miles south, they thought they'd found a dead man. He lay bloated and cold in a tangle of sea kelp, gnats and flies swarming his bruised face and hands. They were startled when he opened his eyes and began his nervous blinking.

"Look, he's trying to wake up," one fisherman said, before another observed, "He's an Indian. Where's Indians this time of year but Digger Bend? We must take him there."

Indeed, his wife expected the worst after he hadn't returned by morning. And when the fishermen arrived and unloaded his limp body from their truck bed, dragging him from between stacks of empty metal crab traps, she, too, thought he was dead. "Lay him there," she said, pointing to his bedroll. A few of the others had seen the fishermen arrive, heard the news, and now stood alongside the helpless wife. She saw the rise and fall of his chest and his blinking eyes, but it wasn't until a woman said out loud, "We must do something. He's still alive," that she realized she wasn't kneeling alongside a ghost.

"No hospital in these parts will take a dying Indian," a man warned.

Someone remembered that a crew of Indians from Lake

County was working in the hop fields near Windsor, and among them was an Indian doctor. They sent for him, and he arrived that evening sometime after dinner. No one played cards or gossiped around the fires, not so much because each and every one of them believed in the old medicine ways but out of respect for the sick man and his distressed wife.

"All I can do is sing," the Indian doctor said. "If he makes it by morning—even if he is only still blinking—then he will live."

He gently touched the thin man's bloodied hands and his slashed ear. He studied his swollen face, saw the lump on the thin man's forehead where he'd crashed into the rock. Then he began to sing. He sang until the morning star shone in the sky, and then, without another word, began to pack his cocoon rattle and clapper stick ready to leave.

"Wait!" the thin man's wife exclaimed, and she reached for the cigar box she'd pulled from the gunnysack the night before to remind her husband of his foolishness once he'd returned.

"No," said the Indian doctor. "Don't touch that cigar box. Let your husband open it."

"You're right," she answered, embarrassed, "there's nothing in it anyway but junk. I was thinking of money, where I might find something to offer you."

"I'll take that there." He was pointing to what was left of her torn dress in a ball on the ground. "My wife can make a beautiful quilt."

She handed him the dress, embarrassed now that the torn dress was all he wanted.

During the night, many of the onlookers had fallen asleep, and shortly after breakfast everyone left the camp for work.

Midway through morning the thin man sat up.

"I must tell you where I've been," he told his astonished wife.

At first, she thought he was merely describing his trip downriver, but before long she was thoroughly confused.

He'd traveled downriver as he had three times before, he said, when, in no time, he found himself at the mouth of the river, and not just that but he was in the air and able to see the ocean as far as the horizon. Then at once he was turned, looking eastward, able to track the Russian River to its headwaters. He thought at this point that he was sitting in a chair, but when he looked he saw he was on a branch high in a tree, his legs dangling in the air. The branch was thin, no thicker than his arm, and he wondered how it would hold him without breaking. But then he was seeing upriver, seeing the camp at Digger Bend, where a man was headed downriver, pushing through the brush.

It was him. He watched himself staring at the tiny green stone in the palm of his hand. Not a minute later he was under the pool of water seeing hundreds of fat salmon, but after attempting to corral all of them against the opposite shore, there he was out of the river with only a tiny catfish. Farther downriver he flew until he found himself under an oak tree. In his cupped hand was the ace-shaped acorn. Not a second later did he see his head inside the tree's large trunk. All the while, the tree's branches were full of ripe acorns, which he could now see from his new vantage point. Finally, bloodied and exhausted, he was at last looking directly down at himself standing on the ocean's edge near the mouth of the river. "No," he told himself. "No." But it was too late, for already the ocean's ebb tide was carrying him inexorably toward the rock. He began to cry in shame, choking out the word "foolish."

But it was not the thin man who spoke. Across from him on a pine branch was the osprey. The poor thin man became incredibly frightened, thinking the osprey, now the size of a man, might cause him to fall from the tree.

"Please," the thin man begged, "don't let me fall."

Now he saw himself just as the osprey had seen him.

"I got greedy, thinking I could impress the others with a hundred or more salmon. I thought I'd be able to beat the big mustached man at cards. I thought I'd capture more and larger abalones than anyone before me. And I thought you would help me find the box of gold. And now I see what you have shown me." The thin man then began to cry in shame and embarrassment. "I forgot to take only what I need. I forgot to play fair. I thought I could take shortcuts. What was I thinking? All those guys who returned from the war with new cars and houses . . . All those fancy things they brag about . . . I thought I'd show them up. I thought I'd finally impress my poor wife."

"Foolish," the osprey repeated.

The thin man then saw that he had two feathers in his hand. "What are these?" he asked the osprey.

"One feather from each of my wings."

"What am I supposed to do with them?"

"You tell me," the osprey answered and then was gone.

His wife scratched her head. "Then what happened?" she asked him.

"That was all."

"So, you had a dream."

"If it was a dream, it was as real as you and me sitting across from one another." Then, after a moment, he said, "The osprey gave me two feathers."

"Yes, you told me," his wife sighed. But in that moment she also noticed that her husband, though still bandaged, appeared to be wide awake and not still dreaming, and she was surprised that he showed none of his usual nervous habits. He wasn't blinking rapidly, and he wasn't biting his lip or twitching his arms.

"I flew at last, using these long arms," he said.

"I think you'd better rest," she told him. "There was an Indian doctor here last night who sang for you. Everyone saw you were near death. Fishermen brought you back from Bodega Bay. Do you remember any of that? So, rest."

"No," he answered, easily getting to his feet. "Dear wife, it is daytime; I must get to work."

Just as he was leaving, he caught sight of the cigar box next to the gunnysack. "No need for those things in that cigar box anymore," he told her. "I've learned my lesson."

She handed him the cigar box. "The Indian doctor said that you were the only one to open it."

He opened the box then, and in his hand was the most beautiful necklace either of them had ever seen. It had shiny abalone pendants, an ace-shaped acorn, and a green stone at the center, and, hanging one on each side of the acorn and green stone, there were two osprey feathers, white-and-black striped, what you see as the osprey flies overhead, wings spread.

"Those are the feathers!" he exclaimed. "It is a woman's necklace. It's for you," he said, handing it to her.

She followed him to work as always (for in the crops Indian women worked alongside the men). She questioned what her husband had told her of his travel downriver, not to mention what he'd lifted out of the cigar box. Regarding the necklace, she figured he could have had time away from her to string the abalone shells and the acorn and green stone, but where did he get the feathers? After all, she'd seen the broken pieces of abalone shell, the acorn, and the green stone, but never before the two osprey feathers. Only one thing was certain: her husband was calm and, despite the bandages and bruises, he was working as hard as he ever had.

Alas, after work that night, he returned to the rock, waiting for the osprey. A few of the people laughed and jeered. Others felt sorry for him—and his poor wife.

"He's completely lost his mind," a man said.

"Not even the Indian doctor could help him," a woman said.

"What a fool," the mustached man said. "Ha! He thinks that bird will help him beat me in a card game."

"Or buy him a shiny new car," another man cracked.

"The bird will no more help him win a single hand of cards than it will help him find that lost box of gold," continued the mustached man.

And just then the osprey appeared in the sky and the thin man, instead of following it downriver, immediately turned from the rock and ran to where his wife was sitting alone alongside the gunnysack.

"I've got it! I've got it! I've got the answer for the osprey!"

The poor woman put her face in her hands, fearing the worst of what nonsense might come out of her husband.

"I've got the answer—the answer for what I can tell the osprey."

"Oh, no. What?"

"To remember," he said. "To remember."

He opened the cigar box, put the necklace on his wife, and sat back marveling at its beauty, and how in the firelight the abalone pendants glinted and reflected on her face. She saw again the calm, the peace in her husband, even before she understood what he had just told her—that the osprey feathers were to remind him to think only of what he needed, that otherwise he would forget the rule of taking just what a person needs, not to cheat, always to share. And little did she know then (yet soon enough would she find out) that her husband would become known as the man who always caught enough salmon for friends and family, and who knew where to find plenty of acorns and abalone.

Miraculously, four days later his wounds were completely healed. "I have an idea," his wife said. She washed the scraps of her dress that she'd used for his bandages and made a beautiful blouse, which she then put on and wore with the necklace, astonishing her husband, who saw the oranges and greens and other bright colors of the blouse, which, together with the beautiful necklace on her neck, made the thin man think he saw in her the entire earth.

A week later people packed to leave Digger Bend. The work was done for the harvest season. They continued to both worry for and make fun of the thin man, for, night after night, he continued to wait for the osprey. But his wife knew better. And as the others packed their belongings, proudly opening the trunks of their new cars and bragging about wins or explaining away their losses, she had a smile on her face, and that's why, years later, if people had remembered her and thought to say hello, they'd find the same smile on her face as she stood down at the rock marking Digger Bend.

Part Four

"Sister, that poor thin man," Question Woman said. "His head got so full with ideas he couldn't think."

"And thinking is what he needed to do to remember," answered Answer Woman.

"That's how my head gets when it's too full of questions. It actually hurts."

"That's when you need stories. The best cure for a headache."

The sisters, perched on the fence, took in the wide view of the valley, its cities and towns, below the mountain. The sun rose higher in the sky. The air was pure. It was morning yet.

Then Answer Woman saw her sister scratching her head.

"Oh, no, here comes a question," she said.

"Gee, you're smart."

"Just observant."

"I'm thinking about the osprey in the story. Is that what ospreys do? Is that their purpose, to show humans their foibles?"

"Ospreys, like all of Creation, have many purposes, all depending on whatever their unique abilities and talents are. Ospreys go up and down the river, just as the thin man's wife said. They fish. The thin man was searching for luck—he was being foolish—up and down the river. The osprey gave to him his gift of the long view of the river."

"What else can ospreys do?"

"Lots of things, but not everything. No one creature or plant or rock on this earth can do everything. We need each other; that's what the Forgetters forget. Which reminds me of a story . . ."

"What do you mean?"

"This talk about animal powers and the Forgetters reminds me of another story."

"What story?"

"It's about a woman who met an owl, a rattlesnake, and a hummingbird in Santa Rosa."

"What about her?"

"Listen."

A Woman Meets an Owl, a Rattlesnake, and a Hummingbird in Santa Rosa

elow the hills east of Santa Rosa there was a village called
Kobe·cha. In the Southern Pomo language, *kobe* is rock and
cha is house. The village sat on a knoll above a deep blue
pond. It was a good place to live. Fish—bluegill and catfish—
in the pond, and plenty of acorns and deer in the hills. What
distinguished the village was its triad of enormous rocks, which
were connected one to another atop the knoll. Passersby farther
west on the plain might see the plumes of fire smoke and, following it, find these rocks and the villagers scurrying about below
them, small as rabbits or birds. Kobe·cha, they'd say. Rock House.
A small creek snaking below the hills fed the pond. Sometimes,
with heavy rains, the creek swelled and the pond rose until the
knoll was an island. But the villagers didn't worry. Until there
was another great flood, when the ocean itself would rise again,
Kobe·cha would not be covered by water. More rain, more grass
for the deer and elk, they said. An early American farmer dyna-
mited one end of the pond, hoping to capture the winter rains,
but it was a developer building tract homes who finally accomplished the deed, installing drains that caught the water on street
corners.

It was around this time, say the early 1950s, that Isabel was on the other side of Santa Rosa picking strawberries. It was May and it had been unusually hot for at least a week. Each second seemed endless, as if the sun had stopped time. Thick scarves covered the women's heads, straw hats and sombreros for the men, but as they bent over the rows and rows of strawberries, heat found their backs and shoulders, baked their skin under their clothes. Filipinos and Mexicans, poor whites, and Indians from different rancherias worked in the strawberry fields. Isabel was an Indian. She was twenty-five and plain, which meant she did nothing to call attention to herself. If anyone was to talk about her, they might claim that her unwillingness to dress up after work each night or to cut her hair fashionably was the reason she still wasn't married. Others might say she was just quiet by nature and respectful. Still others might say she was shy. Whatever the case, she minded her own business.

Sometime in the afternoon, as Isabel was filling her crate with fruit, a large ripe strawberry slipped away from her. She reached down, but just as she was clasping it between her thumb and forefinger, it scurried under a green leaf as if it were a mouse or a lizard. She figured she hadn't really seen what she had seen. She was just tired. Maybe the sun was too hot, or maybe she'd eaten too much for lunch or hadn't had enough water. She straightened and took a deep breath. She wasn't dizzy. When she reached for the berry a second time, again it escaped her. Again and again she went after it, and each time her fingers touched the fruit, it was gone, only to be discovered under yet another leaf. She went for water, letting the flow from an irrigation faucet at the edge

of the field run over her face. Refreshed, she returned to where
she had left off, and she pulled her crate along, easily picking
berries one after the other, hurrying down one row of plants and
up the next, for she had no sense of how much time she'd lost
and knew she needed to make a daily quota for the farmer to
pay her.

That night as folks gathered around fires telling stories and
listening to the pockmarked Mexican with a silver mustache
play his accordion, Isabel thought about what had happened
that afternoon. She figured something had gotten in her eyes,
temporarily blurring her vision, or that indeed she had been
dehydrated and her mind was playing tricks on her. As she dozed
under the stars—no one slept inside the tents on account of the
warm weather—she listened as the sounds of voices and laughter blended with the melodic notes of the accordion. But all the
while, she thought about the strawberry escaping her and felt the
sensation of it slipping from her fingers. She looked about and
it was day again, and she was still reaching for the strawberry.
Water glinted in drops on the tops of her hands, and there was
nothing else but the folks' voices and the Mexican man's music
in the sky above her. But she was not asleep. She was wide awake.

The next morning, and throughout the day, she felt alert and
awake, despite the sun, which, unbeknownst to her, was even
hotter than before. She worked, bent over the strawberries, picking the red fruit, up one row and down the next. Only when the
farmer arrived before lunch with metal barrels of fresh water did
she realize how warm the morning had already been.

"I don't want you to have to keep drinking that dirty slosh from the field faucet," he said.

Isabel watched the men and women filling canteens and gallon glass jugs with water. Then, lest she look like a sick animal left behind in an empty pasture, she joined them. Up close, she saw the sun glistening on the water inside the glass jugs. She felt a strange attraction to the water, or maybe to the reflected sun, she couldn't tell which, but she was certain that whichever she reached for, the water or the reflection, it would escape her, slip from her hand, just as the strawberry had yesterday afternoon. She filled her canteen, though she truly wasn't thirsty.

That night, wide awake, thinking of the strawberry and the glistening water, she overheard someone mention Kobe·cha and the deep blue pond while telling a story, and right then, perhaps for no other reason than to distract herself from the pictures that kept repeating themselves in her mind, she determined to go to Kobe·cha, knowing full well that she would have to leave camp in the dark and return before daybreak, lest anyone notice she was gone or, worse, find her late for work and think she'd been out with a man someplace.

It was a three-mile trek across town. It was dark. There was a full moon, but it was low in the western sky and pale, like a yellow button on a black dress. She went up Farmers Lane and turned west on Fourth Street, then east, following the line of hills above town. She knew where Kobe·cha was but found herself lost in a maze of new streets and houses where only last fall she'd picked walnuts. She was stopped, ready to turn back, when she suddenly realized that she was standing on a street corner where there were once clover fields, that the maze of new streets and houses now covered the Jersey dairy also, for she could see the landmark that was Kobe·cha's three enormous rocks, two and three stories high, and, dwarfed below them, the dairyman's farmhouse. She remembered from picking walnuts that folks had pitched their tents near Kobe·cha. Now, following a street and then a dirt path, she found the place again and kept going until she was stopped by the remnants of a barbed wire fence—all that was left of the dairy besides the farmer's house. But from where she was standing, looking eastward, she could not see the house, only the rocks, yes, enormous, shaped like the huts of a giants' village.

She was surprised that in the dark she could see so well, the shapes of the rocks, the outlines of the trees, the water. She looked about for a streetlamp, though she knew she wasn't close to a street corner, and then she saw the moon, not where she remembered it, low in the sky, but directly above her, not a yellow button but a full white orb giving form to everything she saw, and reflected so large on the pond that it seemed the orb in the sky could just as easily have been a reflection of the one in the water.

She thought that she probably just hadn't been paying attention when she'd noticed the moon earlier, that she'd been rushing to find her way. She looked behind herself now, up the dirt path, and when she turned back to Kobe·cha she half expected the light to be gone. But it wasn't. Then she realized she was out of time. She figured it was close to dawn, that she wouldn't make it back to camp without being discovered, and as she hurried along

Fourth Street and then Farmers Lane, she felt she'd been foolish, completely mindless, and she resolved never to leave camp in the middle of the night again. And yet the next night, no sooner had the Mexican retired his accordion—before even the fires were coals—then she was gone.

She found herself stopped by the barbed wire fence, just as before. She heard voices and wondered if someone had seen her leave camp, or maybe had spied her from a window in one of the new homes and followed her. But the voices, soft, yet clear even from where she was standing, came from below the rocks, she was certain of it. She stepped through an opening in the leaning fence and made her way to the rocks, avoiding gopher holes and low-growing shrubs that might snag her clothes with stickers. The going was easy, for it was bright again, moonlight over the trees and on the water. The rocks were huge, truly enormous. Standing at their feet, she could not see their tops. And because she was staring upward, she did not at first see, silhouetted in the moonlight, the three figures seated on the ground below her: a woman and two men.

When she noticed them, her breath caught, but she was more embarrassed than frightened, as if she'd found herself inside a camp uninvited.

"I'm sorry," was all she managed to say.

"Don't be," said the woman, who then pointed to an open space in the circle. "Make yourself at home."

Isabel thought the woman might be making fun of her, maybe merely displaying the perfunctory kindness old timers showed strangers. But these three people weren't old, and perhaps not all were Indian. The unusual light that was everywhere shone on them as bright as the sun. Isabel guessed they were close to her own age, in their twenties, and they wore contemporary clothes, the woman a sweater over a housedress, and the men jeans and long-sleeved shirts. One man was an Indian, but the other two Isabel wasn't sure of. The woman's hair, parted on the side, was wavy, betraying Spanish or Mexican heritage. The other man was light-skinned, and he could well enough have been white. With Isabel's arrival, they'd stopped talking, but when they started again now, seeming oblivious to her sitting among them, Isabel found that what she'd interrupted was a story they were telling.

"Waterbug wanted to kiss Quail Woman," said the Indian man.

". . . and when he saw her take a drink of water, he wanted to know the water's song so he could enchant her to kiss him," added the woman.

". . . so, he stole the creek and wouldn't return it until he forced the song out of the creek," continued the light-skinned man.

And then, Isabel thought as she listened, the mountain and everything all around dried up. There were no salmon in the creek. People were dying of thirst. Until Eagle, Waterbug's ex-wife, took him in her talons high into the sky and forced him to spit out the song and return the creek, and then Eagle dropped Waterbug so that when he hit the ground his legs bent clear around, which is why, to this day, he goes about the creek water backward.

It was the story of how Waterbug stole Copeland Creek. Isabel knew the story. When the woman said, "Yes," Isabel thought that perhaps the woman had been reading her mind or, far worse, that she herself had finished the story out loud.

Amidst the silence that followed, Isabel grew more and more embarrassed, convinced that she had been rude.

"It's an ancient story from Sonoma Mountain when the animals were still people," Isabel said.

If she *hadn't* finished the story out loud, she thought one of them might show surprise at her contribution, and if she *had* finished the story out loud, she figured one of them might comment on or respond to what she said. But no one said a thing. More and more, Isabel felt as if she were in a dream.

She spoke again: "You told the story because we are next to the pond at Kobe·cha and the water is dammed up. The white people trapped it—like Waterbug with Copeland Creek."

She said it as much to herself as to the three people in the circle with her.

"We tell lots of stories," the woman said. "Wherever we go."

It was then that Isabel saw that the light on the three faces was beginning to fade, and the people appeared to be retreating from her, and all she could think was to hurry back to camp.

All the next day she thought about the three people. She wondered if indeed she had met anyone, for the more she pondered, the more she felt she had been dreaming. She'd behaved badly, she thought, hadn't introduced herself but chatted on as if she'd known them forever. Were they workers who'd wandered from a camp nearby? The only crop this time of year was strawberries, and she didn't know of any other strawberry farms nearby. Maybe they worked on a dairy; there were still plenty of dairies west of town. She seemed to recall that the light-skinned man and the woman were seated together, that perhaps they were a couple. She told herself that she wanted to see if what she remembered was true. It wasn't that she was nosey about them but that she needed proof they were actual people, that she had walked to Kobe·cha in the middle of the night and hadn't been dreaming.

That night, she headed out again, but when she reached the leaning barbed wire fence, she forgot whatever reason she'd given herself for rushing across town in the dark. When she came upon the three people, they seemed just as before, but not one of them said a word to her. They gave the impression that they were familiar with her, that introductions had long passed, and that they had merely paused mid-conversation. But Isabel was anxious, and alarmed that already she could see them so clearly, a circle of light upon their faces brighter than the full moonlight.

"Who are you?" she asked. Hearing herself, she could not believe her complete lack of manners, but then, just as she opened her mouth to introduce herself, the woman spoke.

"Hummingbird," the woman said.

Isabel figured Hummingbird was a nickname. But no sooner had she heard the woman speak than she felt momentarily disoriented, even lost. She knew enough Southern Pomo to know the word for hummingbird, and enough English and Spanish too, but now she could not remember what language the woman had spoken. Again, she wondered if the woman was Mexican or Spanish. Then the woman leaned into the light-skinned man next to her.

"You know who he is," she said to Isabel. "Yes, we are married."

Isabel's earlier impression was correct: they are a couple.

"I'm Rattlesnake," the light-skinned man said.

Isabel grinned. Certainly, they were joking with her. She knew the story from the time on Sonoma Mountain when the animals were still people. Men competed for Hummingbird's heart. Fox offered Bobcat, Hummingbird's father, mounds of acorns, enough to feed Bobcat for one winter. Skunk offered fresh blackberries, Raccoon a beautiful flicker-feather headdress, and Mountain Lion a bow and sharp obsidian arrows. Rattlesnake, a rather ordinary man, had only a song to offer, and it was over her father's objections that Hummingbird chose Rattlesnake, for the song benefited not just her or her father but the entire village. Rattlesnake's song called the crickets up Sonoma Mountain each fall so that, hearing the crickets, the villagers knew to prepare for winter.

"I know the story," Isabel said, laughing out loud now. "Yes, Rattlesnake and Hummingbird got married. She knew he thought of other people; that's why she picked him."

Then the Indian-looking man said, "I'm Owl."

And Isabel was confused.

"What does Owl have to do with the story?" she asked.

"Well, nothing with that particular story," answered the woman.

"But all of the stories are connected, like all of Creation," added the light-skinned man. "That's what we must remember."

"So, I call you Owl?" Isabel asked the Indian-looking man.

"And me Hummingbird," the woman said.

"Rattlesnake here," her husband said.

Isabel felt that they'd all been playing, that she'd only joined in their joking. But with the silence that followed, she soon became uncomfortable.

"Yes," said the man who called himself Owl, finally answering her question. "I'm Owl." Then he asked her, "How do you think you got here?"

"And back to camp both nights so fast?" added Rattlesnake.

"You use my eyes to see at night and my wings to move silently and swiftly," said Owl.

"You use my wings so that you don't get tired," said Hummingbird. "Oh, and during the day too."

"You have my mouth so you don't get thirsty," said Rattlesnake. "And during the day too."

Isabel had to admit that, since seeing the three people, she hadn't been thirsty during the day, or at night, for that matter. For the last two nights, she'd gone to Kobe·cha and back to camp with ease, never discovered by anyone, whether from the camp or one of the new neighborhoods. These realizations made her feel uneasy, and suddenly she felt trapped. If this were a game she had been playing with them, it wasn't a game of her own making.

"Why me?" she asked. "I don't want any special powers. I don't want favors."

"That's good enough reason alone," said Hummingbird.

"Yes, we see that you are a good person," said Owl. He spoke as if he'd just concluded a long study of her.

Rattlesnake shrugged. "You came here, what more?"

Because she didn't know what else to say, Isabel said, "Well, at least I know the story," and already the light on the three faces was beginning to fade, and then before she knew it Isabel was making her way back to camp, only to return to Kobe·cha the next night just as fast.

They were there. The light on their faces was so bright that, even before she reached the leaning barbed wire fence, she could see they were waiting for her. She took for granted now the strange occurrence of the full moon, each night unchanged in the sky and on the pond's surface, for, if anything, it reinforced the strange feeling she had of being in a place and time she hadn't known before. During the day, she doubted this feeling, her memories of the nights before, even as she was telling herself to drink though she was never thirsty, asking herself how the three strangers at Kobe·cha knew the ancient stories. Two of them didn't look like Indians. And hadn't she forgotten to ask them where they were from? A work camp? A dairy?

"Who are you?" she now blurted, forgetting her manners.

"We told you," answered the woman calling herself Hummingbird.

"No, I mean really, who are you?"

They looked at one another confused, as if she'd spoken a language they didn't understand.

"Do you work on a dairy?" Isabel asked, seeing their confusion.

"No," answered Hummingbird.

"We just go about," said her husband, Rattlesnake.

"Well, actually, we can work anywhere," added Owl.

Once again Isabel felt as if she were being played with, and she was determined to get answers to her questions. She didn't want to insult them, inquiring about their physical appearance, but she couldn't help herself.

"Are you Indian?" she asked.

"I am," answered Owl.

"I'm mixed with Mexican," answered Hummingbird.

"I'm Irish and some German," answered Rattlesnake.

Isabel wasn't satisfied. Now more than ever she felt she was being made fun of, that what they were saying wasn't true.

"Are you witches of some kind? Or poisoners or human bears? If you're looking to recruit me, I don't want to join you. I don't want to do any bad things. I'm not mad at anyone. I don't want to take vengeance on anyone, and I'm not jealous of anyone," Isabel continued, remembering stories of how a witch might recruit an unwitting young person.

Owl, seeing Isabel's increasing frustration, leaned forward so she could hear him clearly. "We tell stories."

"That's all we've ever done," Rattlesnake said.

"Of course, at the same time, we've become the stories ourselves," added Hummingbird.

"But each of you isn't all Indian," Isabel said.

"Anyone can become a story," Owl answered. "An old story or a new story."

"Isn't that all anyone becomes?" said Rattlesnake.

"We're just old stories in new human bodies," said Hummingbird.

Already Isabel had begun to feel more comfortable, for even as her mind continued to whirl with questions, she could see their concern to help her understand.

"We're as old as the rocks here," Owl said.

"You don't look old," Isabel said.

"We don't grow old," Hummingbird said.

Then Hummingbird started telling a story, and, after her, Rattlesnake, and then another told by Owl.

Isabel returned again and again to Kobe·cha. She listened to stories, proud that she knew so many of them, and charmed by the ones she heard for the first time. She was proud, too, of her special abilities, none more than that she could escape at night unseen, as if her secret were itself a power she could hold over the others. Which was why, returning one early morning, she was frightened out of her wits to find a man silhouetted under the streetlamp at the corner of Fourth Street and Farmers Lane. At first she thought he might be Owl or Rattlesnake playing a trick on her, perhaps acting the part of a story they'd told her. But he wasn't. As she drew closer, she saw the man was Rodrigo, the work camp supervisor, her cousin's husband.

"My friends and I know where you've been," Rodrigo told her.

Isabel said nothing, but as she followed him back to camp, she felt she was being led in handcuffs.

Apparently, her cousin's husband on his way to the latrine happened to spot Isabel slipping from camp one night. The next night, he waited and watched her, then deployed two of his friends to follow her through the new neighborhoods and as far as the dirt path that led to Kobe·cha.

"So that's how we know where you've been," said her cousin's husband before returning with his two friends to their campfire.

Isabel was frightened they might have seen her below the big rocks, her face and those of her companions lit by the bright light. At the same time, she was furious that they had followed her, for what business of theirs were her whereabouts. In the days ahead, gossip spread through camp, though little was said to her directly. "Do you meet a man there?" asked the cousin whose husband had followed her. An old man snapped at her, "Your people are from Sebastopol, from the lagoon. Kobe·cha is not your ancestral village. What business do you have going there?" and Isabel, though she didn't say anything, had an answer for him: Water is water. It's connected everywhere.

She missed her friends at Kobe·cha, but she wouldn't leave camp lest someone follow her again and discover them. At night, each long minute next to the fire would be proof for those watching her that whatever stories they were telling about the woman who traveled at night to Kobe·cha were now just that: stories. But she was torn. Even as she wanted to protect her friends, she felt betrayed by them, as if in the end she had in fact been foolish enough to believe them. Which was no doubt why, when she found herself again seated among them, she wasn't surprised. She was thinking only to get answers to her question.

"You gave me a mouth so I don't get thirsty," she said to Rattle-snake, and to Hummingbird, "You gave me wings so I don't get tired." Then she looked at Owl. "And you gave me eyes to see at night and wings to move silently and swiftly." She took a deep breath, then let out, "So how did I get caught?"

Owl looked to Hummingbird and Rattlesnake. They appeared confused, just as they had when she'd first asked them who they were, as if she'd spoken a language they didn't understand.

Finally Owl spoke.

"You are not all-powerful. No one is. Have you forgotten the power of humans? They are tricksters. They are clever. That is their power. They can trap anything. They can trap the water. They can trap animals and even one another. But they forget the limits of their power, they do not remember that *they* are not all-powerful, and when they do forget these things, harm and destruction comes. The water dries up. Plants and animals disappear. Isn't that what the stories we've been telling remind us? You got trapped. You thought that, with the gifts you have, you were all-powerful."

Isabel thought of the water trapped in the dreams on every street corner of the new neighborhoods. She thought of the deep blue pond now trapped by steep concrete walls. And wasn't it just a few weeks ago, when they'd first arrived at this camp, that she had witnessed her cousin's husband determined to shoot every last crow eating a strawberry? She felt foolish now. Ha!, she thought to herself, this all started with a strawberry getting away from me, but to her amazement, she'd been speaking out loud, for Hummingbird immediately rejoined, "Oh, it started before that. You just saw it then and started paying attention."

"And you'll always pay attention," added Rattlesnake. "And now you will be able to come back and join us safely."

Isabel thought it was Rattlesnake who kept talking, launching into a story, but she wasn't certain, for the next thing she knew she was awake on her bedroll. The sun was up, and her cousin was saying, "It's late. Get up. Last day of work here, or did you forget?"

Isabel followed her cousin and the others to another work camp, hops, and after that prunes and pears. Whenever she heard talk of her night journey to Kobe·cha, she smiled to herself and merely went on her way. She eventually married an Indian and had three children. People continued to tell stories about a woman at Kobe·cha, eventually without mention of Isabel by name, no doubt because anyone who might have known her from the strawberry camp had passed on. People claim to have seen a woman near the water, and neighbors tell of waking at night to the sound of voices, people talking. Today there is nothing left of the pond but a square of dirty water. Even the rocks are gone, having made way for a swimming pool. Still, it is said the woman is seen there now and then. She looks the same, about twenty-five years old and plain. She never grows old.

Part Five

"The woman in 'A Man Follows an Osprey' grows old. But in the last story, 'A Woman Meets an Owl, a Rattlesnake, and a Hummingbird in Santa Rosa,' the woman, Isabel, gets to live forever," said Question Woman.

"What difference does that make?" asked Answer Woman.

"That's what I'm asking."

"It doesn't matter. In both stories they live forever—that is, as long as we remember them."

"Yes, the stories." Question Woman sighed. "Sister, it keeps happening in the stories, people forgetting things when the answer is right in front of them. Even good people, like Isabel, they can't seem to remember."

"Yes, Question Woman," Answer Woman said before completing her sister's thought. "People focus too much on what they want, or, as with Isabel, they forget the bigger picture. She forgot human beings' charms, the ways in which they can outsmart other people—and animals—and how that can help them, but also hurt them if they don't remember what the stories so often show us."

The two sisters sat a long moment before Question Woman, taking in the long view of the valley below the mountain, sighed again and said, "We continue to tell stories because we forget, isn't that right? And then the silly things we do become yet another story to remind us."

"That's right, Sister."

"So will it ever end, our need to tell stories?"

"Ha! I doubt it. We keep forgetting or, as you say, doing silly things. It's what makes us human. But then we have stories, which is the other thing that makes us human."

Question Woman flapped her wings, stretched, and yawned. "It gets tiring thinking there's no end to stories."

"Not if they're good ones," answered Answer Woman.

Then Question Woman bolted upright, a question filling her head. "Sister, it seems all the Forgetter stories are about Indians. What about all the other people?" She gestured with her shiny black beak to the towns and cities below the mountain. "Those other people wandered longer and farther from the mountain than the Indians here."

"The land can speak to them too, Sister. What is your point?"

"So then tell a story about someone who is not Indian."

"How about the story of the Chilean man who was haunted by a meadowlark? Listen. It's a good one."

Meadowlark Haunts a Chilean Man

This, too, happened in Santa Rosa near Kobe·cha, where there was a dairy, green clover fields, and brown Jersey cows, and east, bordering the dairy, rows and rows of walnut trees. The dairyman lived in a house painted white with red trim near the big rocks of Kobe·cha. The old widow who owned the orchard lived with a maiden sister in a large Victorian overlooking her walnut trees. But before there was a dairy or an orchard, a wide swath of field spread from Santa Rosa Creek to the hills. After winter, after the creek and ponds overflowed, flooding the land, the sun dried the field so that the endless clover and bunchgrass turned the yellow color of morning. That's when, they say, meadowlarks sang all day long there.

The Chilean man milked cows for the dairyman, and he harvested walnuts for the old widow. He told people he'd made the long trip from his native country to work in the sawmill. The Chilean detailed his arduous journey over the Pacific Ocean, telling of numerous shipmates dying of cholera and dysentery. He himself swaddled the bodies in thick sheets before dropping them overboard. He said, too, that he was a nephew of Captain Stephen Smith's wife, Manuela Torres, who some say was Chilean, others Peruvian. Captain Smith, originally from Boston, built and operated the mill located near Bodega Bay, just west of Santa Rosa. Smith died in 1855, and his wife remarried and eventually relocated to San Francisco. Once she left the North Bay, she never returned. That was eighty years ago—too long ago for this Chilean man, who was only thirty years old, to be the nephew of Manuela Torres Smith. It seemed he had grafted himself into a book or story he'd read, without realizing he was outside of time.

He was anxious and he talked incessantly, mostly about his connection to Mrs. Smith and about all the people he'd known on his journey. And he bragged, impressing upon people his numerous talents. He could build a fence and change a tire faster than anyone. He drank wine, and the more he drank the more he talked, louder and louder in Spanish and English and Tagalog, as if his switching languages so quickly fortified his image of a world traveler. But no one saw him nail even a fence rail to a post or change a single tire. He didn't milk cows faster than anyone, and, before long, he was fired from the dairy after, one evening, drunk as he was, he left the cows unmilked, which the dairyman was alerted to by the cows' painful bawling. As for the old widow, when she saw the unhusked walnuts rotting on the ground, she merely looked at the man and then pointed to her gate with a stiff finger, thinking the man didn't speak English but would understand the gesture.

Wherever people gathered you found him, whether at parties or in the evenings around fires in the work camps. Uninvited, he appeared at weddings and joined the circles of gamblers playing cards. Always he talked of his bold adventures and of his friends and relatives, though certainly he seemed to have none of the latter. And who could tell whether or not he had actually swaddled the dead and tossed them into the Pacific Ocean, where whales a hundred feet long followed alongside the ship? Who was alive that could remember anything about his relationship to Captain Stephen Smith's wife? The best you could say was that people tolerated him, at least when he wasn't drinking. Maybe they felt sorry for him. For all his talk of connections in high places, he appeared hardly a pauper or what people in those days, the early fifties, called a hobo, a lost wanderer. He was small in stature, thin, wizened even, and his clothes looked as if they belonged to another person, someone much larger, which only made him look that much smaller.

After a time, he began to annoy people more than they could stand. Once, when he was drunk, he pestered a young girl, and her father chased him into the hills with a gun. This was in the fall when folks were harvesting walnuts for the old widow. He had wandered uninvited into a tent where several Mexican men were playing cards. He had no money to join the game, so he just observed quietly, which is what he'd also done during the day; he'd tried his best to go unnoticed under the walnut trees lest he draw the attention of the old widow, who'd cast him from her orchard. A young girl entered the tent with a plate of warm tortillas, and when he followed her outside, the men, one of whom was the girl's father, assumed the Chilean wanted to beg for a tortilla. "He could've just asked us," the father said. But it seems the Chilean had other intentions and had followed the girl into the tent where she slept with her mother. After he was caught, he claimed he'd only entered the mother's tent to ask the girl to go to the movies with him. But whatever he said or did, what happened next created a stir in the camp, resulting in the father drawing a pistol, all of which was reported to the old widow in the morning. The Chilean was cast out from the community of Mexicans, the only people who spoke his native language.

Not long after, in the hop fields, he tried to impress the Filipino men with a fighting cock, but there was one problem: the rooster wasn't a fighting cock but a prized Rhode Island Red the Chilean had stolen—or "borrowed," he later claimed—from the hop grower's barnyard. "We don't know him," the Filipinos claimed in their defense, and afterward they kept their distance from him. They hurled rocks and dirt clods whenever he came within ten feet of their campfire.

As for the Indians, the Chilean man thought they were dumb, but he also thought that meant the women basket makers he'd seen weaving might give him a few coins if he told them where sedge grew along the Russian River. "Ho!" they chided him. "Get out of here. All you do is cause trouble."

Whatever money he earned he spent on wine. And before long, drunk and with no one to talk to, he was a complete nuisance. He slept on the outskirts of the work camps. He'd become dirty, his clothes tattered and smelling of urine, and passersby would hear him moaning and crying like a coyote prone on his back under a tree. After the sheriff arrived one night and no one claimed him, he disappeared, perhaps arrested for drunkenness, only to be heard again somewhere in the hills at night above Kobe·cha. At first, people thought maybe they were hearing him in their own memories, and they drove their cars to Kobe·cha to listen. What they heard wasn't the moaning or crying as before, but a frantic and desperate howling. The nights had become cold, and the only work left was pruning in the vineyards and apple orchards, but perhaps he had joined a new camp. "Has he found work somewhere in the hills?" people wondered. "But who would keep a man who hollers all night like that?"

Then, all at once, the hills were silent.

"Has that crazy Chilean left us for good?" the crowds asked, for the people had become a crowd as, night after night, more curious workers had gathered near Kobe·cha. "Was he fired from whatever job he had up there?"

They parked their cars and stood along the fence waiting to hear him. They had more time, now that so much of the work in the fields was done. The first frost came and still they parked and talked quietly among themselves, listening for the echoes of a man hollering from beyond the trees. They'd long returned to their homes for winter, but they continued to gather and catch each other up on the day's news and trade stories about where there might be work. After a time, any sound resembling a human calling out would turn into an argument until it was decided that what they'd heard was no more than a cow.

Finally, an Indian and a Filipino decided to search for him. Jackson was the Indian's name, Armando the Filipino's. It's a wonder no one thought to search the hills during daylight. Careful not to trespass on private property, the two men followed the narrow roads where already new homes with stupendous views of the valley hugged the hillsides.

Jackson figured the Chilean had worked raking leaves for one of the homeowners. But he wasn't going to approach the front door of a wealthy white person. "I'll ask for work," Armando offered. "They sometimes hire Filipinos for cooks and permanent gardeners."

"Yes," said Jackson, "maybe they'll tell you if they hired someone or, better yet, you might see the Chilean." But nowhere was the Chilean to be found.

Then, where the road curved just above the dairy barn, the two men were stopped by a meadowlark singing loudly, its bright-yellow breast against the green oak leaves catching their attention. Jackson commented that singing birds should have left Kobe·cha by this time of year, and, thus distracted by the bird, they hadn't noticed, at the base of the tree, the man posed there as still as the rock he was sitting on.

It was a large rock, visible from the dairy fields and walnut orchard, which is why the two men, and eventually the others, were surprised to find the Chilean there, since they could see him perched atop it so plainly now that they knew where to look. He appeared small, like a bird or some other animal, as he sat peering out, seemingly at the valley below, where the people lived. He made no sign that he saw them, and no one traveled into the hills to approach him. "Best to let him be," they said, "or he might start screaming again." What no one said (but everyone thought) was that the entire scene was strange. Why hadn't they noticed him sooner, and now having found him, why was he so still and quiet? And the meadowlark kept singing, loud enough to be heard clear across the field and through the orchard. The Chilean sat day and night, and the bird sang far past dusk.

When it began to rain and puddles filled the low-lying fields, he was still there. It was winter, the days short. "This certainly isn't normal," people were saying, their speculations soon going wild. What was especially alarming was that now, in the middle of winter, when meadowlarks should have long migrated else-where, the bird was still there, somewhere in the tree, its voice still loud over the land. Eventually, a few people felt sorry for the Chilean, figuring he was wet and cold, and someone got the courage to ask if he wanted or needed anything. The Chilean said nothing but, surprisingly, he followed the person down the hill.

He *was* wet and cold—and he was hungry. What had he been eating anyway? Now, Filipino men took him in and fed him rice and chicken adobo. He ate, but he never said a word. He sat star-ing during the day, and at night he slept stretched out on a bed-roll on the floor. That is, if he slept. Even in the dark, his eyes were wide open. This man, this Chilean, was not the person the people had known before.

"He's had a stroke," a Mexican woman offered.

"Maybe someone beat him," one of the Filipino men rejoined. "Why else would he have been screaming in the hills? Has any-one checked to see if he's bruised or has any broken bones?"

But the Chilean wasn't silent for long.

His Filipino hosts were awakened in the middle of one night with a bellowing so loud the walls of their house shook. Plates fell from the kitchen table, pictures from the walls. "My wife's letter from the Philippines fell into the fire," one man complained. The Filipinos, frightened that neighbors would call the sheriff to their house, asked a Mexican family if they might at least keep the Chilean in their chicken coop. In this way, he was passed person to person, family to family, each suggesting to the next that he might find peace in a different house.

It was a young Mexican boy who, speaking Spanish to the Chilean, learned in a brief moment between loud screams that the man kept mentioning the bird, nothing but the word *pajaro*, over and over. It was then that people noticed the bird had stopped singing. They thought that the man probably missed the bird, but it wasn't so.

When he all at once spoke, which surprised people, he said the meadowlark was haunting him. He said, between bouts of hollering, and switching back and forth between Spanish and English, "The damn thing won't top talking. It follows me."

They tried to reason with him. They took him back to the rock, pointed to the empty tree, but he said he could still hear it. The best they could do was keep him quiet while they talked to him. But who could talk to him, attempt to reason with him day and night? They took turns keeping him overnight and feeding him. But soon it was they themselves who felt haunted. Even after they had passed the Chilean on to someone else, it was as if he were still following them, if only through their memory of his unmistakable screaming.

Then something happened. It was early spring, and he was with the Indians near Mark West Springs when they were preparing for their first fruits ceremony. Tradition was that someone stood on top of the Roundhouse and called people to the dances.

"Make him useful; he can call loud enough," a woman said, meaning only to joke.

The next thing you know, he was on top of the Roundhouse. At first he just screamed and hollered incoherently, but by the time people were ready to announce the start of the dances, he was calling Indians near and far to the Roundhouse in a loud and clear voice. Also, having assumed the duties of the official announcer, he named every plant and fruit and flower of the new season, for, as it is believed, if you forget each plant and fruit and flower, they will forget the people. Different elders taught him how to call out the names in an orderly manner. He took pains to memorize the names lest he forget a single plant or flower:

Clover.
Live oak.
Valley oak.
Buckeye.
Bulrush.
Sedge.
Wild strawberry.

Some of the Indians at Mark West Springs wondered if it might not be a curse having this Chilean assume such an important traditional role. Others thought the Chilean a mere madman, even as he learned so quickly. He often looked lost, his eyes distant as if he might still be hearing the meadowlark or if, at any moment, he might burst out loud again. But he didn't. He repeated the names of the plants each day, then slept soundly at night.

Even before the four-night spring ceremony was over, people wondered what they would do with him after. So relieved by his silence, they suggested other activities to keep him busy. A Filipino who was married to an Indian woman taught him to make chicken adobo and rice. The Mexicans taught him to play the guitar; he could sing too, and before long he was interpreting their lonesome rancheros about the hardships of life in faraway lands like no one they had heard before. When he eventually returned to work milking cows and then harvesting walnuts, neither the dairyman nor the old widow recognized him.

He pestered no one. At first the Filipino man and his Indian wife who had taught him to cook feared he might start something with their daughters, but what more did he ever do but get busy at the stove and then, just as quickly, wash all the pots and pans after each meal. In fact, he spoke very little and kept busy. On the rare occasion he looked up from his work, his eyes were still distant, as if he were listening to that bird or, worse, at any moment he might start shrieking. After he had enough money from his hard work and moved into a place of his own, people missed him. They told stories about him during the long winter nights, anxiously awaiting the work season, when he'd cook adobo for the entire work camp and sing rancheros so beautifully that, they claimed, he made the stars shimmer in the sky above them.

A housing tract and a strip mall replaced the dairy and walnut orchard. The hop fields too disappeared. The old timers marveled at how a place could change so quickly. "You could be lost here," they'd say. "Our grandchildren will never know orchards and work camps."

Now and then they drive along the streets and past the shiny houses that cover the green clover fields. They park where they can see the rock where the Chilean man sat. The tree is gone. The rock, no doubt too big to remove, decorates the spot like a statue in someone's front lawn. Whatever happened to the Chilean, the old timers aren't certain. Did he go back to Chile? When did he leave the camps? Did he leave all at once or was it gradual, disappearing one season, then appearing the next?

"There," they say, pointing to the rock.

Some still speculate whether or not the man was crazy. The Indians claim the meadowlark possessed him. But it wasn't only the Indians who saw that the man had found peace. Whatever the case, he was lonesome, the old timers agree. Then he listened to the meadowlark and things changed.

Back and forth they go, arguing, even as they agree the Chilean found peace in the end. What happens next is that one of them will tell the story start to finish by recalling even the dairyman's white house with red trim and each of the plants and flowers the Chilean named on top of the Indians' Round-house. Then another old timer will tell the story, attempting to outdo the first with more detail. No one forgets when the meadow-lark enters the story, and here they stop a moment, as if they too can hear the yellow-breasted bird singing in the oak tree's green leaves.

Part Six

After hearing about the meadowlark and the Chilean man, Question Woman sat quiet. Answer Woman, perched alongside her on the fence rail, gazed toward the valley in the distance below the mountain. Of course, Question Woman could not keep still for long.

"Sister," she said. "So much has changed. First, the land before the white people. Then the dairy. Then the dairy was gone, leaving only streets and houses."

"You've left out a lot of other changes along with those changes. What happened to the grizzly bears and wolves, for example. They're gone."

"So, Sister," Question Woman kept on, "I know we can listen to birds, but what if the birds are gone? What if there are no birds, no trees, only barren hills and endless towns and cities? Surprise! Even I know the answer to that question: There's still a story to tell."

"So, do you have another question, or do you want to sit quiet awhile longer?"

"I don't like sitting quiet."

"I've noticed, dear Sister."

Surprisingly, Question Woman remained still. The sun had

shifted, lowered in the sky. Shadows grew below the fence and at the bottoms of the coyote brush and towering anise along the road.

Answer Woman stretched one wing, then the other wing before turning again to her sister. "Look," she said, "stories can take us to a timeless world. They can take us to the past, no matter what is changed or lost, so we might think better now and in the future. My goodness, they take us back to the time of creation on this mountain. That's what happened to the Forgetters when they left the mountain and destroyed so much of the earth and its life. They forgot the stories and fell away from the true world where we are all one family."

"Yes," said Question Woman, coming out of her reverie. She nodded with her beak to the fence shadows. "I've lost track of time. You've been telling stories since morning, and now I see it's past noon."

Suddenly excited, Answer Woman said, "Your talk of losing track of time makes me think of another story. It's about a man who shot his stepfather."

"Did he kill his stepfather?"

"It's more complicated."

"So, what happened?"

"Listen."

A Man Shoots His Stepfather

He was coming back on foot from Marshall, where he'd been courting a Mexican girl named Magdalena. The sun was a red ball low on the horizon, and he had another five miles north before he reached Bodega Bay, where he lived with his mother and stepfather at what remained of the old Indian village Mitca. In those days, the late 1800s, the dirt road he followed above the ocean was so uneven a sturdy wagon had difficulty navigating its ruts and potholes. He listened at every turn for a wagon, or even a lone man on horseback, should he have to hide his shotgun under the long coat he wore. White people thought an Indian carrying a gun only wanted to poach deer or a cow.

When he reached the estero, not far from Bodega Bay, it was dark save for a faint light that lit the water, enough so that he saw the floating silhouettes of ducks, so many that the entire estero was sprinkled with the dark figures. He drew his gun. But as he took aim, he saw at the water's edge hooves, then several sets of deer legs come out from under the willows, and he shot. He heard the thud of an animal hitting the ground, but after he waded across the marshy water, he found nothing. The ducks were gone too.

He continued on his way. He was tired. It had been a long

day. He had hardly impressed Magdalena with his new shotgun and fancy overcoat, much less her father. He could have bagged several ducks had he not been distracted by the deer, and now what did he have to show for himself but wet clothes? The ducks, wings flapping in the dark sky overhead, mocked him. This run of bad luck he would easily have forgotten if he hadn't found his mother the next morning, tweezers in hand, extracting buckshot from his stepfather's side.

She had her back to him, kneeling before her husband, who sat bare-chested on a chair. Watching from the doorway, the man at first had no idea what his mother was doing, perhaps mending her husband's pants. He thought she was pitiful, a scarf-headed Indian old before her time. She cooked food over an open fire. She'd never used a stove. His stepfather, though seemingly younger, square-shouldered and taut, wasn't much different, for how could he accept that his wife and stepson live in a window-less shack with no more than a dirt floor when any man these days with even the smallest amount of pride would provide windows if not also a wooden floor for his family?

A lantern sat atop an upturned apple crate. When at last his mother straightened and turned, she held a pair of tweezers mid-air long enough for him to see in the flickering light what they held. He saw it was a buckshot pellet, and then she dropped it onto the apple crate. Seeing the buckshot called to mind what had happened the day and night before, and he didn't want to think about it, all of his bad luck.

He went north to the mouth of Salmon Creek, where he could

dig clams. When the steam mill was open, he hadn't minded working there for a salary, but since it had closed down, he had little to do aside from digging clams, and to him it now felt like a form of punishment. And he couldn't even make any money that way. White people didn't pay for clams, so there wasn't anything else to do with clams but sit by the fire and eat them with his mother and stepfather. For money, an Indian man could only find seasonal work in the crops, and although Indian women often worked regular jobs as housekeepers, his mother did not. She cleaned and cooked at home. How often he found her, the stepfather alongside her, staring out to the ocean or up into the hills. It was hard enough for him to be Indian, worse that his family was lazy, which no doubt had influenced Magdalena's polite rejection of his advances the day before. And speaking of lazy, his stepfather somehow had the energy to steal a lamb or pig, but then he was stupid enough to get caught, which was what again came to mind the next morning, when his mother gingerly held another buckshot pellet in her tweezers before dropping it atop the apple crate.

The next morning, another pellet. On the fourth morning of this, thinking his mother either too lazy or not smart enough to extract the buckshot at one sitting, he said out loud to his stepfather, "You shouldn't have got caught. You'll be in that chair the rest of your life before she gets the last pellet."

His mother looked at him and then back to her husband before slowly picking up the pellet from the apple crate with her tweezers and holding it midair, as if in a show of defiance.

Each morning, one more pellet, only one. He began to feel persecuted, that they were attempting to trick him, that his stepfather wasn't shot at all. But why would they be tricking him? Did his stepfather somehow know that he had shot at the deer? Were both his stepfather and his mother trying to teach him a lesson, that he'd been compulsive and not honored the deer before he shot? Were they making fun of him because the deer got away? He was mad at himself for returning to watch their ritual. Frustrated, he walked into the dark shack and, looking over his mother's shoulder, saw that indeed his stepfather was wounded. A map of welts, either open and bloody or gray with the color of a buried pellet, covered his chest and abdomen. He thought again how careless his stepfather was to get caught stealing from a white man. Having neither a gun or even a decent knife, he couldn't have killed the animal first, then made a silent getaway. No, he had probably used his bare hands to hold the squealing piglet or bleating lamb. Maybe he had even been dumb enough to carry off a calf. But before the man could say anything, his wounded stepfather looked up at him, saying only, "Someone shot me."

He wasn't surprised that his stepfather would utter the obvious. But now, after a week of his mother's daily extractions, even that simple answer felt loaded. When he asked, "Where were you shot?" and his stepfather told him, "Down by the estero," he was stunned, then enraged. What game were both of them playing with him? And how could he have not seen the man somewhere in the willows behind the deer? Had his stepfather seen him, and

if he hadn't, why didn't he call out after he was shot? He must
have been well enough to call out if he were well enough to walk a
mile or more home. Confused, the man left the shack and vowed
not to go back the next morning, much less admit that he had
shot his stepfather. Wasn't that what they were waiting for him
to do? Why else would they be playing this game unless he had
shot his stepfather?

His anger grew as he asked more questions that he couldn't
answer. The thought occurred to him that he hadn't harmed his
stepfather, that the lazy man had been shot by someone else, perhaps earlier in the day, and so maybe they weren't blaming him.
After all, only a white man would fire so quickly at an Indian.
The two Italian brothers who owned that portion of the estero
allowed Indians to fish there, never bothered if the people of
Mitca or anywhere else trapped ducks with nets. Had the brothers shot at his stepfather because they had heard the man shoot
at the deer and become alarmed? He was the one who had shot
the gun, but he wasn't the one who'd shot his stepfather. And so
why did his mother keep holding up the buckshot for him to see?
Why not just say one of the Italian brothers shot his stepfather?
Nothing made sense. Night and day, whatever questions he asked
or however he answered them, what remained in his mind's eye
was a pellet held midair in his mother's tweezers for him to see.

People in the village noticed that he began to do strange
things. Each day, he traveled to the estero and returned with as
much willow as he could carry, not just fine long branches that
he might use to make a trap but entire portions of a tree that

he would leave in the center of the village. The villagers didn't know what he was thinking, and he didn't want them to know either, for he was ashamed of his thoughts. He wondered if his stepfather might want him to believe that he, the stepfather, was a walepú.

The man thought of the ducks he'd heard after he'd left the estero. Loud ducks, the raucous singing of birds, such were the signs of a walepú, a shapeshifter waiting somewhere in the brush, perhaps behind a tree, who had transformed himself or herself into an animal, oftentimes still partly human, with only the face of the shapeshifter. A story was told of a girl who'd seen a walepú. She was walking home after school with an armful of apples when she heard a sudden loud chorus of birds. She fell into a spell of forgetfulness that could only be cured by the striped-face man she'd spotted in the bushes after hearing the birds. Most people these days considered them devils—that is if they believed such things. The man wondered if he was imagining that he had heard ducks, or if it had been perhaps a coincidence that he was only now remembering them. Besides, as the story was told, walepús transformed themselves deep in the redwoods overlooking Bodega Bay, but those trees were now gone.

When he traveled to the estero every day, what he was looking for was a skin. A walepú who had been shot with an arrow or a bullet often left a skin behind, and the wound would be visible in the abandoned hide. The man wanted to prove to himself— particularly if his mother and stepfather for some reason were playing a game with him—that there was nothing under the willows. If there was no skin left on the ground where he'd shot at the deer, then there was no walepú. Wasn't that what was happening? Did his stepfather want him to think there was a walepú, or even that his stepfather himself was a walepú, if only to scare his stepson and teach him a lesson? And so the man went to the estero every day, and he would bring back the willow cuttings and stack them in the village, not only to prove to himself that he'd scoured the estero for a skin but, at the same time, to prove to his mother and stepfather that he'd done so and wasn't afraid of anything they might be trying to do. Soon the entire willow grove, in cut branches and tree trunks, was piled in the center of the village. Then a second willow grove and a third. People could hardly locate the front doors of their homes. They built fires a safe distance from the village and no longer cooked inside, for fear a spark anywhere might ignite the mountain of drying willow trees.

When the Italian brothers appeared on the outskirts of the village one morning wondering why this man was cutting down their trees, the villagers couldn't answer, much less explain why the trees were piled so high in the village. They worried that the next time the brothers returned they would have the sheriff with them. They bade the man to stay away from the estero, where for many years the brothers had allowed them to fish and trap ducks.

He didn't return to the estero. Whether or not he'd heard the Italian brothers and, like the others, was afraid of the sheriff, nobody knew. He talked to no one. He worked day and night cutting pathways through the piled willows. Because the trees died and the branches crumbled, he found that just as he finished his work at one end of the village he would have to start again at the other. People wondered if he thought he was helping them to find their homes amidst the piled trees. But again, he didn't talk, so they had no answers. He was unapproachable, lost in his thoughts. He didn't see them or seem to know where it was in the village he was working. On the rare occasion he rested, he gazed up into the hills, and when his mother offered him a cup of water one afternoon, he, rather than thanking her, said as if admonishing her for a lie, "There are no trees in the hills. No birds sing."

He lost weight. His cheeks hollowed; his distant eyes bulged. He became more and more unapproachable, frightening even. One old man told the villagers that the man needed an Indian doctor, that he was possessed by some evil spirit or that someone had poisoned him, perhaps another Indian who had eyes for the Mexican girl Magdalena. Another villager thought he'd been bitten by a rabid animal, maybe at the estero, which would explain why he'd returned to the estero and, in his madness to find the animal, began chopping down all the trees.

Three more times his mother offered him water. The fifth time, just as he handed the empty cup back to her, he was surprised to find his stepfather next to her. And they were suddenly inside the windowless house. He was sitting on the dirt floor, and they were sitting on the two chairs. His first thought was that he needed to get back to the work, that he'd been resting too long. The lamp flickered on the apple crate, and he expected to see his mother holding a pellet with her tweezers in the light. Her hands instead were folded in her lap. He felt he was in a dream, but it was worse that he had no idea when it started. It was as if he'd passed through a thick but invisible fog that he could not return from. When he looked at his stepfather, he saw that he was shirtless as before, but his chest and abdomen were now smooth, without a trace of a single wound.

He figured his mother had tricked him to get him inside the house. He'd been dehydrated, which no doubt had caused him to follow her into the house for water and was now causing his hallucinations. He blinked, focusing his eyes, assuring himself that he had somehow come into his mother and stepfather's house on his own power. But as he stood to leave, he found two women standing behind him blocking the doorway. He pushed his way past them. Outside it was dark, further confusing him. He was certain that it had been at least the middle of the day or maybe late afternoon when his mother had brought him a cup of water. He looked at the dark, empty sky. The night air was soundless. He tore back into the house. "When did I fall asleep?" he said to no one in particular.

He was standing in the center of the room. The lamplight flickered on the walls. He looked at the two women, then turned to his mother, certain now he had fallen asleep after she had led him into the house.

"I see you," she said.

She was looking at her hands folded in her lap. It startled him that, by looking at her empty hands, she was showing him she'd

known that he was going to ask her where the buckshot pellets
went. Now she was looking at him. He turned to the two women,
and before he started for the door again, he thought he recognized one of them, a wizened old Indian with a scarf on her head
whom his mother and stepfather talked to in the apple orchards.

He told himself that indeed he'd fallen asleep, and that during
that time the visitors had arrived. In the event they had played
a trick on him led by his mother and stepfather, he would tell
them hello and goodnight before returning to his bedroll outside, where he'd been sleeping after he'd seen his mother holding
the first pellet. Inside now the two women were seated in chairs,
forming with his mother and stepfather a loose circle. He didn't
remember them having extra chairs. He wondered where they'd
come from and glanced around the room. That was when he saw
the lamp's flickering shadows not on the batten board walls but
on the giant trunks of trees. They were in a redwood forest.

"Aren't you tired of working so hard?" the old woman asked.

He didn't recognize the other woman, but he noticed that she
was younger and pretty, which made him remember Magdalena
and his trip from Marshall. He wished he could start over.

"How long do you want to keep working so hard?" the old
woman repeated. "Look at yourself."

She handed him a mirror large enough to see himself. He felt
his heart turn in his chest with disbelief. He was seeing the face
of a very old man, sunken cheeks, bulging eyes, ravaged skin the
blue color of a corpse. The young girl was looking at him. They
were all looking at him.

"Wake me up!" he yelled. He turned to his mother, "How do I wake up?"

The dream was the only thing he knew now. He could not remember what he'd left behind, only that he wanted to return. "Please," he begged his mother.

She handed him a small, beautifully made woodpecker-feather basket, into which she had placed the pellets she'd taken from his stepfather's chest and abdomen.

"There are forty of them in there," his stepfather said.

"Take ten and put them in your pocket," the young woman told him, "and return the willows to the estero."

"Each and every branch and leaf," the old woman said.

"Then wait by the water until they turn green and grow," his mother said. "Before you return, place the pellets in a small hole."

He took in the thick redwood trunks and anchored himself. Then he left.

Each and every branch and leaf he gathered and carried the distance to the estero. One slow step after another he dragged the heavy trunks. He worked until someone said, "Don't take the driftwood, we need the driftwood for fire," and, driftwood being all that was left, he sat down on the south side of the estero, where he could look north and see the redwood-covered hills while he waited for the willows to turn green and grow.

Seasons changed. Years passed. When at last the willows reached high above the water and covered the banks, he took the pellets from his pocket and placed them in a shallow hole. Then he crossed the estero and, passing through Mitca, made his way into the hills.

"All right," he said, "I've done what you told me."

He didn't wait for them to answer. He picked up the mirror and, seeing himself still a decrepit old man, shouted, "What more do I have to do?"

They were sitting as before, the two women and his mother and stepfather. His mother handed him the beautiful woodpecker-feather basket.

"There are thirty pellets left," his stepfather said.

"Take ten, put them in your pocket, and then wait," the young woman told him. "Put them in the hole when the ducks return to the water."

"Each and every duck," the old woman said.

"Look, I've already sat by the estero a hundred years," he protested. "No wonder I look the same."

"Not long enough," the old woman chuckled.

"Oh," his stepfather interjected and, with pity in his voice, offered, "I have a song—a water song. Water gives life and will help attract ducks to the estero."

"Please, teach it to me."

"Clearly, you forgot the song. It's what helped return the water to Copeland Creek after Waterbug stole the water. Remember, up on Sonoma Mountain when the animals were still people?"

"Please, just teach me the song if it will work and make me young again."

His stepfather sang:

Bending to me
You see your love
Bending to me
You see your eyes wide open

Everywhere I go
Everywhere I go
Like that
Like that
Hey-hey-hey-hey

Off the man went with ten more pellets and the water song. He sat by the water as before. He sang and sang. One duck and then another landed on the water. Spring arrived. More ducks came, and they nested in the reeds under the willows. Clutches of ducklings followed the hens into the water. Another round of seasons passed, and then another. When he saw the estero with floating ducks as far as he could see, he dropped the ten pellets into the same hole as before and returned to the two women and his mother and stepfather, anxious to pick up the mirror. Alas, he was still a horrid sight.

He threw down the mirror. "Now what do I have to do?" he shrieked in protest.

His mother handed him the beautiful woodpecker-feather basket.

"There are twenty pellets left," his stepfather said.

"How long is this going to go on?" he asked.

His mother and stepfather and the two women looked at each other in disbelief at such a question, before the young woman said, "Take ten and put them in your pocket, and wait until you see deer come out from under the willows."

He grabbed ten pellets and stomped out, his mother calling after him, "Remember to leave the pellets in the hole."

For the longest time, he sat looking across the estero at the willows lining the water. Day and night he waited. He watched the water rise each winter, then recede with summer. Ducklings emerged from the nests in the reeds, following their mothers each spring, and then each fall flying into the horizon. He was certain that the two women and his mother and stepfather would play their game forever. By the time he saw deer come out from the willows, hooves and long legs before their bodies, he felt another hundred years had passed.

"What are you trying to do to me?" he asked, feeling helpless. "I've sat at least three hundred years."

His mother handed him the beautiful woodpecker-feather basket.

"There are ten pellets left," his stepfather said.

"Wait," he protested. "Please wait. How long do I have to sit at the estero? Please, how much longer?"

"There are ten pellets left," his stepfather repeated.

"I saw the deer," he told them. "They were deer, not walepú. Is that what I was supposed to see?" He looked at his stepfather. "Am I being punished for thinking you are a walepú? Or am I being punished for not seeing you under the willows when I shot my gun? I didn't mean to shoot you."

He thought he saw the old woman chuckle and the young woman giggle. Even though he felt humiliated, he said nothing. He looked at his mother. She was serene as she held out the basket to him.

The young woman said, "Take the last ten pellets and go to the estero," and the older woman added, "And this time take the basket with you. When you arrive, dig up the buried pellets and place all forty of them in the basket. Then leave the basket in the hole until it is time for you to come back."

Once he arrived at the estero, he thought to himself, How will I know when to come back? I will sit by the water for eternity. He did what he was told, gathering the thirty pellets and then placing the basket with all forty pellets into the sandy hole. He sat back then, resting on his elbows, and waited. Seasons passed, years. I give up, he thought to himself. Eternity here will be my fate.

He missed the villagers of Mitca. He wanted to see his stepfather and most of all his mother. Seasons passed before him, as if they were seabirds flying in a line one after the other. Following the hens, ducklings made their way to the water for the first time. Summer passed and it was autumn; the ducklings flew off. The water song would call them back the following spring. In the meantime, the estero fed the willows and the reeds, deer fed there, walked out from under the trees. He could see the redwoods on the hills and know where he was. All that he could see grew and changed, yet it was somehow the same. He took comfort in what he knew. After all, he'd been watching for four hundred years. When he looked to the hole where he had placed the woodpecker-feather basket and pellets, he was surprised to find his loaded shotgun. He saw stars in the sky, not even a sliver of light left on the estero. It was nighttime. He wondered how he'd fallen asleep and thought only to get home.

Walking through the door, he saw first the flickering light from the lamp atop the apple crate. Shadows danced on the windowless batten board walls. His mother and stepfather were there, and the older woman and the young woman. They were sitting in chairs in a loose circle, and there was a chair for him in the middle of the circle. He'd been thinking of Magdalena and how he'd hurried back to Mitca thinking he'd fallen asleep by the estero and was late. But the longer he sat, the more he remembered the beautiful world he had left behind, how the seasons passed year after year, how from the estero he saw the hills covered with redwood trees. The lamplight wasn't reflecting on tree trunks now but on the walls of his mother and stepfather's humble home. He knew where he had been, he saw his journey all at once, and now, seeing himself wildly shooting at the deer coming out from under the willows, he felt only embarrassment at the picture he was seeing of a vainglorious young man. He knew more than he could understand, and he felt content, yet he had to ask, "What happened?"

His mother gestured to the cup of water in his hand. "Take another drink."

His throat was dry, and the water felt good.

"What happened?" he asked again.

"We doctored you," his stepfather said.

"For four hundred years?"

"You were an easy case," the older woman answered.

"It was just one night," the younger woman said.

He remembered then that if a person encountered a walepú, only a walepú could cure them, and he asked, "Am I a walepú?"

"No," his stepfather answered. "Not yet. You pick animals, birds, whatever, and with them transform yourself. Now you have seen what a walepú sees, that all of time and creation is connected. The walepú remembers the stories from Sonoma Mountain, when all the animals were still people, and he knows nothing has changed."

"I didn't mean to shoot you," he told his stepfather.

He looked then at the older woman and the younger woman before turning to his mother and asking, "Are all of you walepú, even you, Mother?"

"You never ask a person that," she told him. "You will only know if you are a walepú. In the meantime, what you have learned is enough. If people know or even suspect a walepú these days, they will cast the person away, even kill the person. This is the age of the Forgetters."

People today think of Mitca. Seeing a pile of driftwood south of Salmon Creek, they ask one another if they have found the place of the long-ago village. Those who remember the man who shot his stepfather might keep the story to themselves, not let others know what's on their mind as they gaze south to the estero or east to the hills above Bodega Bay. Those who talk usually end the story with his mother's words. They don't want to say more, least of all speculate who the man might be or what became of him, lest he have descendants. A few add that, as his mother spoke of the Forgetters, he became lonesome for the beautiful world he remembered. But then they stop themselves, and if they add anything, it's only that he was good to his mother and stepfather after that.

Part Seven

"Wait!" exclaimed Question Woman. "So, you and I are walepú? After all, aren't we both crows and humans?"

"Sister, yes, we are both crows and humans, but that doesn't mean we are walepú. Besides, if we were walepú, we wouldn't say so, not while others are listening. We just haven't forgotten the stories."

"But I do forget the stories, and so do you," said Question Woman. "I have to ask you a question so you can remember a story to tell me."

Answer Woman chuckled.

"Why are you laughing at me?"

"I'm laughing at both of us," answered Answer Woman. "That's our story, yours and mine. We need each other. Which is what every story from this wondrous mountain teaches. And what the Forgetters have forgotten."

"Oh, I forgot, we're telling Forgetter Stories, aren't we?" said Question Woman.

"So, ask a question."

"I can't think of one. What should I do?"

"Look around. See the outcropping of rocks on that round hill just below us. See the curve of the hill against the blue sky. Whatever you see can make you ask a question."

"Actually, I'm not looking at the hill. I see Copeland Creek making its way to the Cotati plain. I don't have a question, but Copeland Creek reminds me of the story of the pretty woman and the necklace."

"Yes, the pretty woman didn't think she was worthy of a man."

"It was a love story," remembered Question Woman.

"Yes," answered Answer Woman. "I guess I don't have to tell you that one again."

"Aren't we talking about the Forgetters? Tell a love story about them."

"I already have one in mind."

"So, tell it."

"I will if you give me a chance. You're so impatient."

"What is it?"

"Take a breath and I'll tell you the story of a woman who invents a lover."

"I'm listening."

A Woman Invents a Lover

She was a good woman. That was all anyone could say about her. They didn't have to tell one another how, after her mother died, she took care of her father, cooking his favorite meals and ironing his shirts just as her mother had, only to have him leave her and her seven younger brothers and sisters for a woman from town. She took care of her brothers and sisters, mending their clothes and doing whatever else they needed until, one by one, they grew and left too.

Her name was Marlene. Her mother once told her that she had been named after a movie star, but she couldn't remember who that was. And considering she was an Indian and poor, she had to laugh. Even after she'd opened a roadside fruit stand, earning enough money to provide new clothes and school supplies each fall for her siblings, she had to laugh whenever she thought of her name.

She lived where she had been born, in a three-room house her father had built in the country. The walls needed paint; chickens ran loose and pooped on the front porch. Now, in the late 1940s, after the war, anyone who was anyone had moved to town. Convenience was everything.

Marlene was light-skinned—it was said her mother was

Spanish—and pleasant enough in appearance. She was forty now, the house empty. When she announced one day that she had found a lover, it wasn't her age that surprised her friends, it was that never before had she shown the slightest interest in finding a lover.

They speculated why all of a sudden Marlene was talking about a man. She told of his kindness, his big heart, not to mention that he was over six feet tall and handsome. She wasn't boastful. You'd think she was complimenting a friend or telling the old blind woman from under the bridge to take whatever she needed from the fruit stand. She couldn't contain her excitement. The longer she talked, the more she sounded as if she'd discovered an answer to a puzzle she was destined to solve.

"How do we even know it's a man?" one friend asked.

"Because she said so, stupid," the second friend answered. "I think now that her younger brothers and sisters are gone, she is lonely."

Then the third friend said, "She's been so busy taking care of them, she hasn't had time to think of a man. I'm wondering if she even knows what makes a man handsome. Is he really over six feet tall?"

"That's what I meant," the first friend said. "Could she be making him up? Being alone with no brothers and sisters in the house, her imagination might've gotten the best of her."

"Yes," said the second friend. "She may have invented him."

"Poor dear," said the third friend.

She'd known her three friends since childhood. The first was a single woman like herself, but she was a woman of many lovers. The second, a robust woman married to a baker, coveted clothes she could neither afford nor find sizes large enough to wear. The third friend's husband was a philanderer, and despite her kindness and generosity, she couldn't always contain her deep frustration over her husband, which she might take out on others, as when she snipped about the second friend, "She looks like a hundred pounds of mud in a fifty-pound sack." They lived close to one another in a cluster of small houses between the apple cannery in Sebastopol and the lagoon.

The more Marlene talked about the man, the more he sounded too good to be true. He was, according to her, ten years younger than her, and, not that it wasn't possible that a younger man would fall in love with an older woman, but if she was forty and he was thirty, wouldn't he have already been married, or at least have children to support? What was so great about that? She said he was Mexican and worked in the apples, whether harvesting in the orchards or on the processing line inside the cannery she didn't mention. She said she met him when he purchased a pound of flour at the fruit stand. So he couldn't be rich. Marlene sold flour cheaper than the grocery, and only in small quantities. And if he was Mexican, might he not be a seasonal worker just looking for a good time here while away from a wife and family in Mexico? Alone and inexperienced, was Marlene able to detect a lie?

Marlene's friends grew more desperate for answers. If they were jealous or merely curious, they wouldn't say. They watched

Marlene during the day, taking shifts so they could see whoever bought fruits and vegetables from her, or a pound of flour. They made excuses, bought oranges, a head of lettuce they didn't need. But it was at night that the baker's wife, looking from her parted curtain, saw the light on in Marlene's kitchen and spied the handsome man seated at Marlene's kitchen table.

"Are you sure he wasn't one of my boyfriends?" asked the single friend.

"None of them are handsome," quipped the philanderer's wife.

"Oh, stop it. Now let me tell you what I saw," whispered the baker's wife.

From her window where she could see into Marlene's lighted kitchen, she saw that the man was handsome. And from what she could tell, he did appear younger than Marlene. His hair was black and shiny.

"That doesn't mean he's six feet tall," said the first friend. "If I had seen him I would have been able to tell. After all, I know men."

"Maybe she left her curtain open and had him sit on a pillow to look taller because she knew you would be spying," said the philanderer's wife.

But he was tall, over six feet, which the philanderer's wife saw for herself late one afternoon just as Marlene was closing the fruit stand. She was so befuddled she forgot what excuse she had for stopping. She couldn't take her eyes off the handsome man. Then she looked at Marlene and said, "Potatoes, lots."

Marlene introduced the man, said his name, which, to the

disappointment of her two friends, the philanderer's wife forgot. She didn't hear when Marlene said, "Pay me later. I've closed the cash register." She picked up the twenty-five-pound sack of potatoes Marlene had placed on the counter and left. Only after waiting behind a tree and seeing Marlene padlock the fruit stand door and walk toward her house, hand in hand with the handsome man, did she realize how heavy a twenty-five-pound sack of potatoes is.

That night the three friends huddled before the baker's wife's window, looking out toward Marlene's house, only to find Marlene had closed her curtain.

"She must've known you were spying," complained the philanderer's wife, "and now you've ruined it for all of us."

"And now I can't see if he is one of my boyfriends," lamented the woman of many lovers.

"I bet they're having sex," the baker's wife said, prompting them then to collect closer to the window, as if that might help them see through Marlene's closed curtain.

Moths, attracted by the light, kept hitting the window, which was why Marlene had pulled the curtain. She wanted to keep focused on the man across from her. His hands, folded on the table, were large and strong. She couldn't help but glance down at them, as if his hands and the veins coursing under his skin would confirm for her that he was real. It had all happened so fast. It was as if time had escaped her. In its place were images from the night before that she tried to harden into memories as solid as the apples and oranges she sorted at the fruit stand.

Before she knew it, another day had passed, she was bolting the store's door and he was waiting. His hands were easiest to remember, because she'd tried so hard to study them. And she could see his wide-set eyes across the table. But it was his general look of happiness, seen in the near imperceptible grin he wore, that remained most elusive, and drove her to talk to her friends.

"He's a drunk," said the philanderer's wife, "a happy drunk."

"Are you talking about your husband?" snapped the baker's wife. "I mean, except that this man's not a womanizer."

"I noticed you can't get the zipper of your dress all the way up."

"Oh, stop it you two," said the woman of many lovers, before sighing, then adding, "Maybe he's a dimwit."

Marlene considered what her friends said. They were wrong. The handsome man was not a drunk. Neither was he a dimwit. He stood up straight, with perfect timing he opened the door for her, and his eyes were always clear and bright. His voice, betraying a hint of Spanish accent, was deep and resonant. With precise detail, he described the small mountain village he came from in Mexico. He told of his many brothers and sisters, their names and characteristics. And after she told him of her brothers and sisters, he remembered their names, asking her about each of them, and always mentioning that she had done for them what he wanted to do for his. He was groomed and clean. Always he wore a pressed white shirt, sleeves rolled up neatly above his wrists. His gold-colored watch glinted in the light.

"He has the manners of a Spanish gentleman," Marlene told them. "The family must have status."

Finding their way to the fruit stand at closing time, each of the friends had by now gotten a good look at the handsome man as he waited for Marlene, which enabled the woman of many lovers to quip, "He's dark-skinned. He's too dark to be Spanish; well, much Spanish."

"And Spanish doesn't mean a person is rich. Look at you," snapped the philanderer's wife, and then, after hearing herself, quickly adding, "I mean, all of us have some Spanish blood."

"His clothes certainly show he's respectable," Marlene said then.

"Clothes can fool you," warned the woman of many lovers. "Though I must admit he is well dressed."

"Does he have a shirt that isn't white?" asked the baker's wife.

Marlene kept her curtain pulled tight. She didn't want to be distracted by the moths beating against the window, much less the likelihood that her friends might be watching from the baker's wife's window. Marlene and the handsome man shared meals, one night Marlene preparing food on her stove, the next the handsome man returning after their walks to the lagoon with two steaming plates safely covered by hand-embroidered cloths. And yes, he wore a white shirt, always. The same shoes, the same trousers. He wore a plain brown belt. His watch glinted. His skin was dark.

"You don't know anything about him," the woman of many lovers warned Marlene the next time the friends gathered.

"You're jealous that you haven't got your hands on him," the philanderer's wife said.

"I wouldn't want him. He's too dark."

Marlene, not waiting for the baker's wife to add her two cents, quickly interjected, "The white shirt is what men from his region in Mexico wear when they court a woman. And about his skin color, was not General Vallejo, who once owned this entire valley, a Mexican with dark skin? Oh, and before you say anything about the delicious meals he makes . . ."

But she couldn't finish. The baker's wife interrupted, "He's a mama's boy. His mother cooks you dinner."

"I watched him cook myself," Marlene told her.

But that wasn't true. Marlene was lying. Afterward, she wondered about the food the handsome man placed on her table. What did his kitchen look like? My goodness, she had no idea where he lived. The warm tortillas that came with his meals, had his mother made them? His white shirt was pressed and clean; it looked new each time she saw him. Maybe he had many white shirts. That contented grin that intrigued and charmed her, didn't it betray the confidence of a Spanish gentleman? Just because he was dark didn't mean he was a fieldworker. He had time to groom himself every night and cook. He wasn't tired in the least. Those boys she knew in high school, they tried to put their hands inside her blouse every chance they got, and here he hadn't even kissed her yet. He wasn't out there looking for a good time, as her friends suggested. He was a gentleman. She was the object of a courting ritual her friends would never understand.

Despite her friends' constant retorts, she continued to talk about the man, feeling more and more a need to defend him. Not thinking whether what she said was true or not, she added more detail to each story she told. She described the high quality of his white shirts, the perfect gold of his watch. She said his father kept a stable of Spanish horses, and that he shared a house with a wealthy orchard owner for whom he priced apples. The greater her stories, the greater her friends' caustic remarks. Then, one afternoon, Marlene stopped herself and didn't utter another word. The philanderer's wife mocked, "My lover this, my lover that. At least you're so old you won't get pregnant." It occurred to Marlene that it wasn't the man she needed to defend as much as herself. Hadn't her friends all along really been saying something about *her*?

She looked in the mirror.

She was older. Maybe her few strands of gray hair didn't show in the evening sun after she closed the fruit stand, or under the lamplight at the dinner table. A packet of hair color from the drug store could hide the gray. Powder would cover the lines on her forehead, rouge would soften her cheeks, lipstick for her lips. Her hair had to be cut then, fashionably, in a way that wouldn't diminish her brightened face. She admonished herself for not doing more about her appearance, forgetting, if not plain taking for granted, that a handsome man was interested in her.

She and her lover continued their walks to the lagoon before dinner, and after dinner, if the moon was full, he would gaze on its reflection on the water and tell her that the same moon that sees the two of them sees his family in Mexico.

"Yes!" she exclaimed.

But she hadn't really heard what he had said. She was imagining his kiss, imagining that when she had said "yes," she was giving him permission to kiss her.

Recently, she felt like she hardly knew what he was saying, nor did she know what happened each time they were together. The man grew taller. His father's horses were white stallions. Alone, after she told him goodnight at the door, he didn't grow smaller but somehow more distant. She found his place setting at the table, but even then she wasn't certain he'd been there. She told herself she had questions she needed him to answer; she wondered if she had known the answers but had forgotten. But face-to-face with him she always stopped herself—thankfully, she thought, for prying into his life would be improper, a challenge to her worth in his eyes.

She penned up the chickens. She scrubbed the porch. Then she began painting her small house, white with yellow trim, colors she'd seen on a new house in town. With her savings, she bought modern furniture and a double bed. She hung pictures of exotic landscapes on the walls. Her brothers offered to help with the house, but she shooed them away, just as she'd done with her sisters, who offered to keep the fruit stand open after she began closing it at noon. She bought new clothes, bright colors she thought would catch the handsome man's eye. The man, however, grew more distant, not just as he disappeared beyond her front door at night but even while he was sitting across from her at the kitchen table. She was face-to-face with a ghost. Where did he live? Did he have a wife and family in Mexico? Why did they only hold hands? Why didn't he kiss her? She kept a list of

questions she wrote under her placemat at the table, as if to remind herself to get the answers she needed, but still she stopped
herself. She tried harder and harder to see him, but the more she
looked, the farther away he was. One night, unable to control
herself, she grabbed ahold of him just as he was turning to step
off her porch, and, clinging with all her might, she forced her lips
onto his, only to find in the next instant that what she was holding was nothing but the dark night.

"All those clothes and that new hair just made her look older,"
said the philanderer's wife.

"Maybe he was nearsighted and couldn't see how old she was,"
said the baker's wife, prompting the woman of many lovers to
add, "Until he was close enough to kiss her. An old face would
certainly have made him leave."

"And since you're not getting any younger, you would certainly know," snapped the philanderer's wife.

The handsome man didn't return. Marlene's friends took
turns waiting to see if he showed up at the fruit stand, and then,
after Marlene continued to keep her curtain closed, they hid behind her chicken coop, only to watch her leave her house each
morning and return at night alone.

Marlene never told her brothers and sisters why she had
painted the house and bought new furniture. She'd never told
them about the handsome man. One morning, before she left
for the fruit stand, her seven brothers and sisters came to see her.
They were concerned, they said, that her heart had been broken.
Outraged, she hollered, "You don't know the story! Now get out

of my house and don't come back. Good-bye!" And an hour later she was at the fruit stand, grabbing a bundle of carrots from the philanderer's wife's hands and telling her, "You gossiping witch. You and the other two gossipers come into my fruit stand again and I'll call the police."

Her mood became darker and darker, her temper so quick, that in short time her only customers were construction workers and salesmen passing through who didn't know her.

The rains came early that year, one storm after another. The lagoon rose and flooded the roads. In November, water covered the bridge, all access to Sebastopol cut off. The town closed. That her fresh produce rotted didn't bother Marlene as much as the rising water. The deep puddles she waded through didn't bother or concern her either. The water had a life of its own, reaching closer and closer to her, no different, it seemed, from the baker's wife watching from her window or from behind the chicken coop. She felt haunted and angry. Which was why, feeling a presence behind her one night as she locked the fruit stand door, she hollered over her shoulder, "Go away! Leave me alone!" It was after a particularly hard downpour, and she had gone out because she needed potatoes for a stew. When she turned around, she found more than puddles of water: a shadowy figure stood before her. It was the old blind woman.

She was at first surprised, then unnerved that someone who knew her had dared approach. "What are you doing here?" she snapped.

Then she felt stupid and suddenly ashamed. The old blind woman lived under the bridge. The floodwater had covered the bridge. It was cold and dark. The old woman, her feet submerged in water, stood small and hunched. Her clothes were rags. A scarf, sideways on her head, barely covered her face and hair. Marlene took her hand and led her out of the water.

"You are a good woman," the old blind woman said.

"Let me get you something to eat. Isn't that what you want?"

Marlene unlocked the fruit stand door and returned with a loaf of bread and a packet of cracked walnuts taped to the bread wrapper. The old blind woman didn't take the offering but instead pushed at Marlene's wrist so that Marlene would hear what she was telling her. "I see that you are a good woman."

"I used to be," Marlene said.

How can a blind person see anything? Marlene thought. She laughed inwardly at the irony. She felt then a need to clarify what she had said. "I used to be happy."

"You'll be happy again," the old blind woman said. "You'll see."

Marlene again thought of the irony of an old blind woman seeing anything. She figured the old woman was being grateful for the food, but when she attempted to hand her the loaf of bread and cracked walnuts, the old woman pushed back again. The longer Marlene stood with the old woman, the more she felt something begin to unwind inside of her. Marlene was feeling her own loneliness. How long had it been since she had talked to anyone? She felt the old woman's warm hand on her wrist.

"How will I be happy again?" Marlene asked, if for no other reason than to keep the old woman from leaving.

"I'll give you instructions," the old woman answered. Then she said, "The rains will end in February. The water will be low

enough for you to see a square rock large enough to sit. You'll find
the rock easy enough where the reeds part to the lagoon. Each
month afterward, seven months altogether, you must return and
find the next rock where the water has gone down. Mark the
months by the full moon."

"I have seven brothers and sisters," Marlene said.

"Yes," said the old woman.

"But the rains don't always end in February," Marlene questioned. "The lagoon could flood again."

"Ah, that's the second part of the instructions. Water is the
blood of all life. We must take care of it. Rain feeds the creeks
and the river. The creeks and river are connected to the lagoon.
Didn't you get angry at the water for rising?"

Marlene, embarrassed, didn't answer.

"The water will roll back enough for you to find the rock in
February, but only if you go each full moon until then and make
an offering."

"What do I offer?"

"Anything. It's a kindness." The old woman laughed. "Bread,
nuts."

Marlene, suddenly remembering what she was holding,
couldn't think fast enough before the old blind woman took the
loaf of bread and the cracked walnuts and was gone.

It was December then. Marlene waited for the full moon.
Though it continued to rain, the lagoon drew back. On a cloud-
less night, when Marlene could see that the moon was full,
she dropped a loaf of bread, one slice at a time, into the water,

watching as the bread floated and bobbed. Then, because the moon's reflection was so bright, Marlene lost sight of the bread, as if the enormous round disc had swallowed each slice whole.

The rains let up and the lagoon retreated, just as the old blind woman had said. Two more months passed, and February's full moon began to wane. Marlene felt she had made peace with the water, as if she and the lagoon had come to an agreement. The moon's reflection offered solace. She followed the old blind woman's instructions, if only to keep the woman visiting with her each time she came to the fruit stand. Since the old blind woman always appeared near the end of the day, Marlene began to keep the fruit stand open longer for the woman's convenience.

Marlene figured the seven rocks the old blind woman described had something to do with her seven brothers and sisters, but when she inquired whether or not she was right, the woman only shrugged and began talking again about the importance of water and how the lagoon connected the river and creeks. Which was why, when Marlene found herself sitting on the first rock under a full moon, she felt silly. What was she supposed to do? The rock was where the reeds part to the lagoon. And it was square and large enough to sit on. She could think of nothing but her brothers and sisters, and so what else could she do but start looking for clues that had something to do with the oldest, a brother a year younger than herself. When she thought of him, she remembered only that a warm bowl of oatmeal with raisins could resolve any argument with him. She sat and sat thinking of him, but nothing else came to mind.

"So, what does that mean?" Marlene asked the old blind woman.

"Same as me," she answered, looking at the fresh cut oranges and apples Marlene had handed her. "It's a kindness."

Marlene mailed a letter to her brother simply asking him to stop by the house. Her heart raced with trepidation and embarrassment. Not long after, he was at her door, and Marlene had a bowl of warm oatmeal with raisins waiting for him on the kitchen table. He laughed, embarrassed as he recalled his youthful arguments with her. They talked about his school years, the time she sewed by hand a letterman's sweater for him, his numerous girlfriends. She asked about his wife and children.

Then it was March. The frogs about the lagoon sang so loud Marlene was certain their chorus had pulled the full moon to the water. A sister was next in the line after her brother. In second grade she had failed math, but after Marlene taught her to play cards, she could add faster than a sixth grader. So, it was a deck of cards that waited on the table when the sister came to visit. And in April, for the sister who followed the card player, Marlene placed a flower-patterned scarf on the table, remembering how the sister was so grateful for the gift of a flower-patterned scarf one Christmas. In May, she remembered buying her brother a bicycle, and when he came to visit, Marlene had parked on her front porch a new bicycle, not for him but for his son. And in June, she found in an old cookbook the recipe for a blackberry cobbler her freckle-faced sister craved, and then on the kitchen table she served it with a bowl of vanilla ice cream.

"She's let her hair grow out. She doesn't keep herself up any-more," said the baker's wife.

"She had to realize that all she would ever be was plain," rejoined the woman of many lovers.

"Heartbreak will do that to you," added the philanderer's wife.

"You would know, after what that husband of yours has done to you," quipped the baker's wife, who couldn't help herself.

After hearing that Marlene had become her old self, they had each gone into the store. One by one, Marlene apologized to them for having been hateful with her remarks. She made no excuses for herself. She didn't care about what they might or might not be saying about her. It was July. Now that it was the middle of summer, the lagoon was low. She could see the sixth rock protruding from the water, in line with the others. The weather was warm. Marlene had watched the seasons change, winter to spring, spring to summer. At night, after the chorus of frogs, came the owls and the night herons. The grass grew. Blossoms appeared everywhere, followed by wild fruit and seed pods. The more the lagoon lowered, the more Marlene thought about the creeks and river that fed the lagoon. She made offerings of bread. Daytime, fish came to the surface for the bread. Nighttime, she imagined them swimming under the moon. She wanted them to live. She wanted enough water. She remembered that the old Indian women dug sedge root for their baskets and also to keep the edges of the lagoon clean. With a garden trowel, she cleared the sedge and reeds on either side of the rocks. It was for her another offering. She felt more and more that the lagoon wasn't only a friend but a part of her.

"Who are you?" she asked the old blind woman one day as she handed her a cluster of bananas and dried apricots. "I mean, where do you come from? Are you an Indian?"

Marlene felt ashamed for asking about what was none of her business.

"I come from over there," the old woman answered, nodding over her shoulder, "near Cotati."

"I feel like I'm in a story," Marlene said.

"You are. We all are," the old blind woman told her. "Our lives are stories that have been told before. They are ancient stories from the time before this one, when the animals were still people on Sonoma Mountain." She nodded over her shoulder again and then looked back at Marlene and took the bananas and dried apricots. "Now get to work. You have two more months to complete my instructions."

Marlene's grandmother told old-time stories from Sonoma Mountain, but Marlene had forgotten the stories, her childhood long past. Thinking about what the old blind woman had said, Marlene understood more clearly what she had wanted to tell her. Marlene felt timeless.

One afternoon, as she weighed flour into one-pound sacks, Marlene recalled a story about a woman and a man. It was an old-time story. She recalled that the woman had been shortsighted when it came to the man, but she couldn't remember the ending or anything else about the story. A chill ran through her. Could it have been that somehow the old blind woman was looking at Marlene and remembering the same story? Had the gossiping friends talked loud enough for the old woman to hear? Marlene hadn't considered that the old woman would have known about the handsome man. Whenever she thought of him, she was ashamed of herself and how she had acted. She recalled her dyed hair and painted face. She was embarrassed at the thought of seeing him again. She had forgiven herself. She had learned the hard lesson that what the ears hear and what the eyes take in can get a person in trouble. She'd listened to others and not her own heart. She'd lost herself and invented a lover. She wondered if she ever really knew the man. How could she ask him then to forgive her? Take the lesson, she told herself. Never repeat that foolishness. What the old woman had prophesied was true. Marlene was happy. Her family had come back, including the youngest brother and sister, for whom she had not yet provided a special remembrance. They all celebrated birthdays together again. No one missed a Sunday brunch at Marlene's.

She couldn't contain her laughter watching her youngest brother devour the liver and onions she prepared for him, bacon fat oozing from the corners of his mouth just the same as when he was ten. She'd hardly sat down on the sixth rock when that memory came to her. And before the next full moon, she knew what to do for the last sibling. A coconut cake. The sister had adored the coconut cake Marlene had made for her sixteenth birthday. Marlene found the recipe and bought the ingredients in preparation for her sister's visit. But when Marlene stopped to think, she was confused about one thing: when she had sat down to think of each of her brothers and sisters, the memories specific to them had come only after she'd sat on the next rock in line. For her youngest sister, though, she had the memory but had not yet sat on the rock. Nevertheless, Marlene had every intention of completing the old blind woman's instructions and figured there was more she'd learn once she went to the lagoon. Still, she needed to talk to the old woman about something.

"People must make sure there is water," the old blind woman said. "There must be water enough to reflect the full moon. Otherwise, the gifts the lagoon gives to you and all of the world will be forgotten." That was all she said.

Marlene remembered that the next Sunday was her sister's birthday, and the family would gather for the party. She was surprised she'd almost forgotten the date. She was further surprised that, until she sat on the rock, she hadn't thought of the candles she needed for her sister's cake. An image of the tiny flames came to the forefront of her mind. She chuckled at herself, wondering at her forgetfulness, even though she had thought of the coconut cake even before sitting on the rock. But mostly she felt relieved. The old blind woman's instructions were complete. A warmth surged through her. She thought again of the candles. Then, all at once, it seemed she had turned around. Yet she felt she was still facing the lagoon. She could see the moon. Only it wasn't the moon. The handsome man was standing there.

She rose to her feet. "What are you doing here?" she asked.

"Back from Mexico," he told her.

But seeing him just as she remembered him the day he walked into the fruit stand wanting a pound of flour, she knew the answer. It was apple season. He worked in the apples. She saw his white shirt. The gold watch. The plain brown belt and shoes. He was a simple man.

He asked if she wanted him to leave, telling her he'd only come to look at the moon.

She didn't answer. He asked about her brothers and sisters. He remembered their names and characteristics. She wanted to answer but found she was saying something else. She remembered how he had told her that the same moon that watched over the two of them and her family here watched over his family in Mexico, and she began naming each of his brothers and sisters and then describing their characteristics and his mother and father too.

When she finished, there was only the sound of crickets and the call of a night heron from the far end of the lagoon. She wanted to explain everything to him, where she'd gone wrong, what she'd done right, but nothing came. She stepped closer to him. She saw what he was seeing. It was enough. She was a good woman.

Part Eight

"So, what happened?" wondered Question Woman. "Did they get married?"

"What do you mean?" asked Answer Woman.

"Did they get married?"

"I don't know," answered Answer Woman. "The story stopped where it was supposed to stop."

"How do you know where a story is supposed to stop?"

"Where it answers a question. In this case, the story stops with what Marlene, the woman who invented a lover, was supposed to remember. These are Forgetter Stories, Sister, meant to remind people of things they may have forgotten. Remember?"

"I'm Question Woman, have you forgotten?"

Answer Woman laughed. "True. I suppose you've already forgotten the story. If you need me to tell it again, I will. But not now. The day is growing late."

Sure enough, shadows stretched longer over the land. The sun was lower in the sky, and a cool breeze foretold the coming of night.

"I want to hear another story," said Question Woman.

"Like what?"

"I don't know. But I was just thinking about how sometimes

a story doesn't turn out so well in the end after people do bad things. Can the story still be a good story?"

"You just tricked me into telling another story, clever one."

"I didn't mean to."

Answer Woman sighed, then told her sister, "I'm remembering the one about a man who learned to smell flowers."

"Oh, tell it!"

"It's on the tip of my tongue. Listen."

A Man Learns to Smell Flowers

There is a patch of land where nothing grows. You can see it, a meadow of flat, dry earth below a cathedral of redwood trees, on a road between the small town of Freestone and Bodega Bay. A long time ago, a magnificent Victorian house stood there, and before that a lush meadow of clover that the Pomo and Coast Miwok Indians remembered and called each in their own language "beautiful place." "What other reason could there be for the clover—and later, at the Victorian, a garden full of flowers that grew so bright and tall—except that the land was rich and the place beautiful?"

An Indian man took care of the garden. The landowner's wife, with whom he worked tending the garden, called him Ramón. But the Indians called him Kaloopis, the Coast Miwok word for hummingbird, though none of the Coast Miwok knew for certain who he was or where he came from. What they knew was that, as he worked, he stooped to smell flowers, his nose inside a rose's petaled bloom or even atop the cushiony crown of a clover blossom outside the garden. Whenever he was asked who he were or where he came from, he only answered, "Kaloopis," as if he were happy enough with the name they had given him. He was light on his feet—here one moment, there the next—moving from one task to another effortlessly, even joyfully, and, they say, that is where his troubles with the others began.

Kaloopis lived alone. There were four other houses outside the landlord's garden. Kaloopis's house was the farthest from the garden, closest to the redwood trees, and it was small, one room, one window. Only a man as slender as Kaloopis, or a child, could fit through its slender door. The Indians, in the 1870s, were long separated from their ancient villages, and they were at the mercy of American landowners for work and a place to live. Often the landowners were cruel. But not Burton Luft and his wife, Mary. They shared the garden's fruit and vegetables, allowed the Indians to hunt in their woods. Burton Luft never bothered the Indian women. The Indians considered themselves lucky. When stopped on the road to town by a sheriff or, worse, a group of drunken men bent on accosting a woman, they said one word, "Luft," and they were safe.

In another house just outside the landlord's garden lived an expert seamstress and her husband, Jaime, and their four children. Their house was closest to Kaloopis's house. After that there were the expert baker and her two adult sons. In the third house was Johnny, otherwise known as Knife Man. He was a butcher (the source, no doubt, of his nickname), and consumption had taken his wife, leaving him with several small children. Henry, otherwise known as Catfish, lived with his wife in the fourth house, closest to the Lufts' garden. Stringy mustache hair fell from either side of his mouth, so no wonder his nickname. He was a handyman, mending fences, painting, and doing other odd jobs. The Lufts' magnificent white house was kept painted, top to bottom, so bright a traveler could see it from miles away, a year-round job for Catfish. He was considered the headman of this tiny village, or what was called Luft Rancheria, though no one had elected him as such. He took direction from Mr. Luft and oversaw the work that was to be done by others. He was a round-faced man and proud, boastful, his wife's stout figure in his eyes a testimony of how much food he could put on the table. And as is often the case with boastful men, he was envious of others. How had Kaloopis ended up working *inside* the garden, close to the magnificent white house and with the landowner's wife? Why not Catfish?

"How is it, Kaloopis, that you work with the lady Mrs. Luft?" asked Catfish one bright day.

Kaloopis was inside the garden, and the two men were speaking over the picket fence that enclosed the flowers and staked tomato vines and gourds. The sun was full on Kaloopis's face, and Catfish wondered how it was he'd never seen Kaloopis so clearly. His skin was smooth and soft, that of a teenage boy, not a man. How old was Kaloopis anyway? His eyes were black and round. They held a reflection of flowers, more colorful even than the reds and whites and yellows of the roses he stood alongside.

Catfish caught himself staring at Kaloopis, and then, mustering a brusque voice, he asked again, "How is it, Kaloopis, that you work so closely with the lady Mrs. Luft?"

Kaloopis answered with his name, "Kaloopis," no different from whenever he was asked who he was or where he came from.

"Why do you stick your nose in all the flowers?" asked Catfish.

"It's my job," answered Kaloopis. With a sweep of his arm, he gestured to the garden. "I take care of the flowers."

Again, an insufficient answer for Catfish.

Frustrated, Catfish could not stop thinking about Kaloopis and wondering how it was that he had charmed the lady of the magnificent house. Catfish himself worked inside the picket fence—he painted the house, after all—but never had he worked alongside Mrs. Luft or, for that matter, Mr. Luft, from whom he learned each morning what chores needed to be accomplished. Catfish worked like the other Indians. And hadn't he seen Kaloopis not only working in the garden with Mrs. Luft but also, more than once, seemingly lost in conversation with her among the roses and sunflowers? My goodness, he'd sat at tea with her on the garden bench.

Kaloopis told stories to the children at night. He sat on a log telling the ancient stories from Sonoma Mountain when the animals were still people, imitating with his voice those of the characters in the stories: Coyote, Crow, Rattlesnake, and Mountain Lion, as well as Hummingbird, for whom he used his everyday voice. Always he had Knife Man's motherless children sit closest to him, knowing that the twists and turns of his stories, the jokes and laughter, were an antidote for that time of night after dinner when the children would miss their mother most.

That night Catfish sat nearby watching Kaloopis.

He saw in the firelight once again how soft Kaloopis's face

was, a mere trace of beard, hair above his lip and under his chin and nowhere else. Yet Catfish could not get a fix on him. For each character Kaloopis imitated for the children, not only did his voice change but his entire appearance altered, and he was first an old man, then, a second later, a philandering forty-year-old, and then a beautiful young maiden.

The next morning, after speaking about the work to be done, Catfish assigned the others to tasks far from the magnificent house while he busied himself around the barn, where he could watch Kaloopis in the garden. And there Kaloopis was as always, among the roses and rows of sunflowers and gourds, halting his work every now and then to smell the flowers. He detected something peculiar about the way Kaloopis stooped over the roses or knelt above the orange gourd flowers on the ground, his nose touching the stamens of each flower, before resuming his weeding and pruning. And Catfish, counting the seconds on his fingers, found Kaloopis gave each bloom the same amount of time. Most peculiar, Catfish thought.

And then something else. The lady Mrs. Luft, though not nearly as much because she wasn't in the garden all the time, also did the same thing. Now, who started this business of smelling flowers, Kaloopis or Mrs. Luft? Doesn't matter, thought Catfish. I can certainly bend over a flower, count five seconds, and then pull a weed or prune an apple tree.

"So, Kaloopis, what would you think of me working in the garden with you and the lady Mrs. Luft?" asked Catfish later that night.

Kaloopis was seated on the old log, the children cross-legged on the ground below him waiting for a story. In the firelight, Catfish saw the children's faces turned on him, surprised and not at all pleased by his intrusion.

"Well, Kaloopis, what do you think?"

Kaloopis shrugged. He looked at Catfish and then back to the children.

"More people to care for the garden is good," Kaloopis answered.

Catfish worked quickly the next morning, finishing his tasks for the day so that he would have time to help in the garden, all of which he explained to Mrs. Luft by way of asking her permission to do so. He waited until he saw her near the picket fence, then rushed from the barn.

At his offer of help, she only shrugged, which irritated Catfish, but not nearly as much as when she answered the same as Kaloopis: "More people to care for the garden is good."

Catfish walked through the gate and began working on his knees alongside Kaloopis, weeding between the rows of carrots and beets. It was when they got to the strawberry patch that Catfish could finally see close up Kaloopis smelling a flower. So busy watching Kaloopis delicately touching the white strawberry blossoms with his nose, and embarrassed that he would have to do the same, he did not see the distance he was from the first blossom he saw, four feet or more, so that when attempting to touch down on the white blossom's tiny yellow stamen, he instead fell face forward on top of the plants, his nose in the dirt. Mrs. Luft had left the garden to gather eggs in the hen house, and if

Kaloopis saw what happened, he said nothing and saved Catfish the embarrassment.

Work went by each day the same: Catfish finished his chores around the barn quickly and then made his way to the garden. He worked along with Kaloopis and Mrs. Luft. Though they never excluded him, they seemed to always find themselves together, just the two of them, on the garden bench, such that Catfish felt his approach would be an invasion of their privacy. How he wanted to know what they were talking about. How he needed answers. He was determined to work in the garden for as long as it took to find what he was looking for. For a time, things seemed well enough, until some weeks later he saw Kaloopis and Mrs. Luft pulling the weeds that he had missed, having been too busy watching them and not what he was doing. And they were smelling flowers he thought he had already smelled. That they didn't mention his failures bothered him all the more.

That night Catfish found Kaloopis once again on the log telling stories. He wanted to ask Kaloopis outright: What is your secret? What makes you and the lady Mrs. Luft such friends? The children, their faces turned in anger, stopped him. They'd had enough of him interrupting the stories. Never mind, thought Catfish as he stomped away. I will know the answer sooner or later. Everyone will know.

In the garden the next day he trailed behind Kaloopis no less than five feet, both men on their knees weeding a patch of dahlias. He was not going to let Kaloopis out of his sight. That's when he heard Kaloopis singing a song.

"What are you singing?" asked Catfish.

Kaloopis, singing and bending to each flower, did not hear him, so Catfish asked again, "What are you singing?"

"For the flowers. It makes them happy."

"Does the lady of this magnificent house know you sing?"

"She listens," answered Kaloopis, returning to his work.

Catfish thought he had the answer. As his stout wife pulled roasted venison from the oven that evening, he began singing Kaloopis's song. He was certain it was a love song.

"What are you singing?" his wife asked as she set the venison on the table and picked up a carving knife.

"Do you feel anything?" Catfish asked her.

Hardly was she able to ask, "What am I supposed to feel?" before she began sneezing uncontrollably. Attempting to cover her nose, she threw up the knife, which landed hardly an inch from Catfish's bare foot.

When at last she stopped sneezing, she asked, "What in the world kind of song is that?"

Catfish, looking from the knife stuck upright in the wooden floor to the venison peppered by his wife's sneezing, couldn't answer.

Then she said, "Anyway, don't sing old Indian songs. We don't believe in all that stuff. We are Catholics now. Those old things are evil, remember?" She wiped her nose on her sleeve. "Now give me the knife."

What she said got Catfish thinking. How easily Kaloopis moves about, he thought. How effortless is his gait inside the garden, particularly as he strolls alongside the lady Mrs. Luft.

Catfish was certain now that something about Kaloopis was not right. He agreed with his wife that Indians didn't believe in that "old stuff," but what came to mind just then was a walepú, a shapeshifter who could turn into any kind of animal or bird and go about, as the old people said, light as a feather. And yes, they sang songs that put spells on people. It made sense, even though Catfish didn't want to believe what he was thinking: Kaloopis was a walepú.

A chill ran through his body. He looked at his wife. Whatever song he had just sung didn't seem to affect her the way it affected Mrs. Luft. The expression of general dissatisfaction his wife wore day in and day out was still there. She hadn't changed in the least.

"What is the matter with you?" she asked then, looking up from the venison she had started carving.

He straightened. "Nothing," he told her.

All the while, he wondered what Kaloopis did with himself after he told stories to the children. Did anyone know where Kaloopis went at night? Catfish was determined to find out.

It didn't take him long to learn Kaloopis did not go home. Well, he went home, maybe for half an hour, but then he slipped into the woods.

With my faith I will not be harmed, Catfish told himself as he prepared to set out. He put a crucifix blessed by the priest into his pocket and followed Kaloopis.

The woods were dark. From one tree to the next, Catfish marked his way by bending down branches, always stopping and looking back to see his trail should he have to hurry and find his way home. He told himself he wasn't afraid. Still, he stopped before long and turned back. He told himself that Kaloopis had too much of a lead on him. Tomorrow night he would follow closer. At least now he knew where Kaloopis slipped into the woods behind the little house with the skinny door.

The more Catfish thought about Kaloopis the more convinced he was that Kaloopis had secrets. If what he was singing in the garden wasn't a love song intended for Mrs. Luft, then it was a song to cast a spell nonetheless. Look what had happened to his wife with the uncontrollable sneezing, caused no doubt because Catfish did not have all the words to the song, a secret a walepú would not share. Using only half or even a small part of the song would cause a person to be cursed by it. A song for the flowers, my foot, thought Catfish. His poor wife sneezed as if she had a garden's worth of pollen stuck up her nose. Wasn't the song, or whatever part of it Catfish heard, a good way for Kaloopis to cover himself, making Catfish think it was for the flowers when, in fact, it was to scare Catfish? But Catfish would not be afraid. He would find the truth about Kaloopis. With the protection of his crucifix, he'd find a walepú meeting place in the woods. He would tell the others—and the Catholic priest. Together they would destroy the secret den and run Kaloopis and whomever else out of the county. Catfish would be a hero.

That next night, Catfish hid behind a large redwood tree opposite Kaloopis's house. Kaloopis stepped out his door and into the woods. Catfish waited a couple minutes, then followed after him. But Catfish, needing to keep bending branches to mark his trail, could not keep up with Kaloopis and only found himself lost again. The forest was dark. The trees were so tall he could not see the sky. He turned and went home. The same thing happened the next night, and the night after that. Night after night the trail grew longer, only to have Kaloopis elude Catfish once more. Catfish wondered if it wasn't Kaloopis's song driving him deeper and deeper into the woods. He felt possessed by something beyond his control.

"Where have you been going at night?" asked his wife. "Last night you weren't home until after midnight."

He needed to tell her the truth, although hardly to reassure her of his faithfulness, for how often had she said, "Who would want to have an affair with a fat-faced slimy Catfish?" More, he wanted her to know where to look for him should Kaloopis and his den of walepú friends murder him. Wasn't it said that a person who followed a walepú would be killed or lost forever?

"Look at how Kaloopis goes about light as a feather," he told his wife, as if to convince her of what he had been thinking.

She didn't need convincing. She'd noticed how comfortable and light on his feet Kaloopis was, but only now did she realize she hadn't thought much about it before. Sure enough, something about Kaloopis was strange. And she told the others. And now they watched too, leaving their work to hide behind the barn, where they could get a closer look at Kaloopis in the garden. Something about Kaloopis wasn't right. How had they not thought about it before?

"I thought he was just a friendly guy," said one of the expert baker's adult sons.

"Yes, maybe he's just a friendly guy and no more," added the other son.

Catfish's wife countered, "We don't truly know where Kaloopis came from. Yes, he was from one of the Mexican ranchos before the Americans took over. Like all of us. But we don't really know who his family is or where his family was from before the missions and the Mexican ranchos. There were many strange Indians in those places. How do we know he's even one of us? Anyone can learn our language."

The expert baker looked from Catfish's wife back to her two sons, then said to the others, "I feel strange now. What if the lady Mrs. Luft is under some spell? Think how I will feel when I bring her bread in the morning."

"Think how I will feel when I have to touch her while I tailor her clothes," said the expert seamstress. "I don't want to be near anyone under a spell."

"Think of me when I have to deliver meat," said Knife Man, the butcher.

"And what if Kaloopis has put a love spell on her and the next thing we know she has a mixed-blood child?" said Catfish's wife. "Mr. Luft will throw us out of here and we'll have no home. I heard about that happening with some Indians in Ukiah."

"I hadn't thought of that," said the expert baker.

"And my children," said Knife Man. "They listen to Kaloopis no different than if their mother were alive to tell them stories."

Looking to her husband, Jaime, the expert seamstress said, "And our poor children."

"Those are old-time stories," Jaime chimed in.

"Listen," said Catfish's wife to the expert baker, "when you deliver the lady Mrs. Luft bread in the morning, watch to see if you notice anything strange. Same with you when you tailor her clothes," she told the expert seamstress.

"And what are you going to do, you who never go to the big house?" snapped the expert seamstress.

"You who don't do much else but eat your husband's food," added the expert baker.

Catfish's wife, aware of the perception that she considered herself privileged, answered, "My husband is risking his life for all of you. Isn't that enough? Isn't he the hero here?"

In the days ahead they continued to watch Kaloopis and Mrs. Luft from the barn. The expert baker and the expert seamstress did their best, despite their fears, to observe Mrs. Luft up close when they visited the house. Yet no one could detect anything different from what they'd known before. They wondered if Mrs. Luft had always been kind and generous. Or had Kaloopis put a spell on her when the Lufts had first settled on the land? One thing was certain: Kaloopis went about light as a feather.

Meanwhile, Catfish went deeper into the woods. Night after night, deeper and deeper. One night, to his surprise, he found himself at the edge of the forest, and from there he could see in the distance a row of houses. How did I get here? he wondered. The houses sat at the northern end of Sebastopol, along the lagoon. He could have made it here in an hour if he'd followed the road from Luft Rancheria. Instead, he'd been traveling for hours, bending branches to mark his path as he chased after Kaloopis. It seemed now that he'd been traveling in circles. He felt lost. Yet he was certain of what he was seeing: the row of houses at the north end of Sebastopol. And then there it was: Kaloopis's trail, visible in the dark through the wet grass. He followed it to the last house, closest to the lagoon, where there was a lantern burning inside the window.

Catfish stopped a short distance from the house. He could see the lagoon, its water black and still under a moonless sky. He wondered for the first time if he shouldn't just stop, turn back. He remembered that a walepú traveled best on moonless nights. Catfish remembered what he'd heard: that walepús killed their enemies, including anyone who might attempt to follow them, and they hid their victims' bodies. Catfish looked at the dark water, then to the lighted window. Was this not a trap, the lighted window a beacon leading him to a sure death? He had always thought he would find Kaloopis in a secret cave or copse of trees. Even though he seemed to be alone, he was certain he was surrounded, certain that Kaloopis and his friends would attack the minute he looked inside the window. Yet, after grabbing ahold of his crucifix and stepping up to the window, nothing could have surprised him more than what he found: Kaloopis and another man seated across from one another at a table having tea.

What confused Catfish all the more was that the other man

was white. His skin was fair. His hair was orange and bushy. Was the white man a further ploy to throw Catfish off? Had Kaloopis seen the bent branches on the trail and known that he was being followed, and did he now want Catfish to think he was only visiting an ordinary white man rather than joining his cohorts? Either way, Kaloopis's cohorts still might attack Catfish as he stood there outside the window.

The room was small. A metal teapot was on the table next to a lamp. Catfish saw Kaloopis reach across the table and place his hand on the other man's arm. Not long after, both men stood up, Kaloopis readying himself to leave, which prompted Catfish to tear away, but not before he saw the two men hug, their necks close on one another's shoulders.

Catfish headed home. Instead of trying to find his way back through the forest, he followed the road. And a good thing, for already light shone above the eastern hills. He wasn't surprised to find Knife Man driving his wagon with a freshly butchered goat for the Lufts from the slaughter yard in town.

"Are you all right?" Knife Man asked him.

"Why?" Catfish asked.

Catfish was lost. He was more confused than ever. That it was already daybreak and that he was on a wagon with Knife Man made no sense.

"He loves a man. He is in love with a man," he told Knife Man.

"Who?" asked Knife Man.

"Kaloopis," Catfish said.

Catfish was certain that he had discovered something, yet somehow he couldn't understand what it was, almost as if what he had witnessed inside the lamplit window had cast a spell on him. He wouldn't remember the ride home or, for that matter, what he had told Knife Man.

But then people started talking.

"Did Catfish already know Kaloopis loved a man?" Knife Man wondered aloud later that morning. "Was that what he was interested to see?"

"What are you saying?" snapped Catfish's stout wife. "That my husband would be interested in such a thing?"

"Calm down," the expert baker told her. "We have to think this through."

"Yes," said the others in unison. "We have to think this through."

"Well, my husband is not a man who would love another man," said Catfish's wife. "He loves me."

"Which must be a trial," quipped the expert baker.

Then one of the expert baker's adult sons said, "I thought he was just a friendly guy," repeating what he had said before, only to catch the sudden suspicious glances of the others, prompting to him to quickly add, "I mean, it makes sense that he's friendly if he's that kind of man, doesn't it?"

"And look how he goes about light on his feet," added his brother, the expert baker's other adult son.

"Well," said Catfish's wife. "We know nothing about Kaloopis, where he comes from. Like I said before, anyone can learn our language. Wherever he came from before, no doubt they threw him out because he was a bad person."

Finally, the expert seamstress spoke. "Listen, he may be that kind of man, what Catfish saw, but walepús go about light on their feet too. Can't that kind of man be a walepú too?"

"Yes, and now we are all stuck with him," said her husband, who had a habit of always agreeing with her.

"He could have put a spell on Mrs. Luft," Catfish's wife cut in. "She could get pregnant, and we would all get thrown out of here."

"Well, if he's that kind of man, I doubt he would want to get her pregnant," said the expert seamstress, chuckling.

"Isn't she a little old for that?" added the expert baker. "She's at least fifty."

"Well, if he's a walepú he could still put a spell on her to make her love him and do whatever he tells her," argued Catfish's wife.

"Never mind all that," said Knife Man. "I just don't want him telling stories to my poor motherless children. It's wrong."

"Mine either," said the expert seamstress. "No matter what he is."

"Mine either," said her husband, Jaime. "No matter what he is."

"I just said that," said his wife.

"Just remember," warned Catfish's wife, "we know nothing about him, where he came from."

All of them agreed aloud. "True."

Meanwhile, Catfish was taking orders from Mr. Luft and had not heard the talk. As he worked in the garden, he avoided

Kaloopis, appalled after what he'd seen, and he was still afraid. Couldn't it be that what he'd seen in the lighted window was a ploy to throw him off until Kaloopis's walepú friends could kill him?

"They were thinking you might be like that," his wife told him after he sat down for lunch.

"A walepú?"

"No, one of those men who likes men."

"What?" Catfish hollered, jumping up from the table. "Who said that? I'll kill him."

"Knife Man."

"I'll kill him."

"Shhh, sit down! Any of them could be thinking that same thing..."

"But Knife Man started it!" Catfish continued to shout.

"I defended you. Now sit down. Of course no one believes that. You are married to me."

Catfish sat down.

"I think we should call the priest," said his wife.

"What, for me?" asked Catfish.

"For all of us. I feel a curse upon us."

Catfish did not return to the garden. He distanced himself from Kaloopis in every way possible. He talked badly about him in front of others. "What was most disgusting was when I saw him kiss the other man," he said. He also said he was not afraid of Kaloopis, and whenever Kaloopis drew near, he spit at him, for the others to see. The children were forbidden to hear Kaloopis tell stories. He was no longer welcome at community meals. For a while, they left a piece of venison or a bowl of acorn mush outside his door. Then nothing. No one knew what he ate.

That winter an unusually thick frost covered the land and lasted until near the end of spring. If the sun was out, Kaloopis could be seen in the garden, smelling the few flowers that withstood the cold. Otherwise, people didn't see him. It was after the frost finally melted that they noticed outside the garden a large patch of barren earth. It was gray and lifeless. Nothing grew there. By the end of summer, it reached to the forest and spread to the edge of the garden.

Catfish's wife called the priest. By this time, talk of Kaloopis loving a man and his being a walepú had rolled itself into one word: curse. The priest told them, "God punishes sins." He made the sign of the cross as he spoke, and then, looking at the barren earth, he made the sign of the cross again.

A second cold winter came, and then another. Kaloopis was not the same. He was no longer light on his feet. He moved slowly. It was proof, the others concluded, that whatever curse he has brought to the land as a result of his sins has finally turned back on him. The priest was right, they repeated to one another, as if celebrating a victory. Publicly, they boasted of their devotion to God. They told one another of the hours spent in prayer, each trying to outdo the next. But privately they accused one another of unworthiness, even blamed each other for the patch of barren earth that continued to spread.

"Knife Man allowed his motherless children to listen to the

devil's stories," Catfish's wife told Catfish. "And the expert seamstress and Jaime, them too. Oh, and think of it, she still touches
Mrs. Luft's clothes."

And the expert seamstress told her husband, Jaime, "Look,
Knife Man delivers meat to that cursed big house where Kaloopis
has his way with Mrs. Luft."

Jaime agreed.

Knife Man, thinking things through alone with his motherless children, concluded that the problems started when Catfish
followed Kaloopis. He remembered how dazed and disoriented
Catfish was when he'd found Catfish on the road that morning.
Wasn't Catfish, then, the first one cursed? And hadn't he brought
that curse back to the land?

The fourth winter was the coldest and the longest. Kaloopis
sat in his narrow doorway wrapped in blankets. Hunched, his
arms drooped at his sides, he had the appearance of a crestfallen
bird. He was gone after that, the narrow door open, his cabin
empty. Near the end of that winter, Mr. Luft took pneumonia
and died. A funeral was held in Santa Rosa. None of the Indians
attended.

They began to bicker openly. Their private accusations they
made public. Insults were hurled. Doors slammed. With the barren earth spread deep into the garden, they wondered what Mrs.
Luft, now a widow, would have left to give them. The sense of a
curse upon them grew, igniting in them a burning weight that
they could not rid themselves of.

The expert seamstress felt herself most put upon, criticized for allowing her children to listen to Kaloopis and for her near daily association with Mrs. Luft, who surely was under Kaloopis's spell. Which is why, if for no other reason than to report back to the others, she asked Mrs. Luft if she felt herself under a spell by Kaloopis.

"Look," the expert seamstress said, nodding to the garden outside as she continued to hem a dress on Mrs. Luft. "He put a curse on all of us. The land is dying. We all know this."

Mrs. Luft broke away from her. An anger never before seen rose in the kind woman.

"You're foolish," she admonished. "All of you. Talk of curses. Ha!"

Her eyes were cold but clear. She turned to the window. All that was left in the garden were cornstalks and gourd vines, a few bare roses, a single tomato plant.

"I know what the curse is," she said, looking back at the expert seamstress. "Now get out of my house and don't come back."

Shortly after, the expert seamstress and her husband, Jaime, and their children left Luft Rancheria. "There's no hope for us here," she told the others. "And anyway, what vegetables are left for us to eat, that is if the cursed woman in the magnificent house would ever deem herself kind enough to share again?" Before long, the expert baker and her two adult sons left too, and then Knife Man with his motherless children, until only Catfish and his stout wife remained.

Mrs. Luft had given him near insurmountable tasks, in

addition to the work he had been covering for the others. She had
him put two floor-to-ceiling windows on the house, one facing
east, the other west. She asked him to carry large flat stones, cre-
ating a path wide enough for a wagon from the house to the well.
She was stern, unforgiving, it seemed. After he parked the wagon
next to the well, she had him move it several times, hitching and
unhitching the horses for no apparent reason. After he finished
the windows, she insisted he stay away from the house. "No, the
house doesn't need painting anymore," she told him. He thought
she might be losing her mind, if not from a curse then from grief
over her late husband.

He grew sick, bloated. His ankles swelled. His back hurt.
With each shovelful of horse manure and barren earth, he saw
himself digging his grave. There was no end. As he dragged his
feet about the horse barn and over the barren earth, he thought
of Kaloopis and wished that he might return. He remembered
the flowers in the garden and the clover meadow beyond.

One night, Catfish's wife said to him, "I have something on
my mind. I've been thinking."

Catfish, tired and worn down from the work left to him
without the others, didn't seem to care what she said. Nor had he
noticed that she seemed joyful, even triumphant. Stout as she
was, she moved surprisingly easily about. She was enthusiastic
even when doing the dishes.

When his stout wife said a second time, "I have something on
my mind. I've been thinking," she stomped her foot and snapped
her fingers.

"What?" he finally asked.

"Remember when we first came here, all of us, and Mr. Luft said one day he would leave his land to the Indians? He and Mrs. Luft have no children. One day she will die. We are the only ones left. What do you think?"

Catfish looked at his wife. She was a stranger to him.

"I give up," he said.

The next morning, he packed their wagon. Together they left Luft Rancheria. Unless she wanted to stay behind alone, she had little choice but to go with him.

The Indian cabins fell to the ground. The magnificent white house faded until it was a gray color, not unlike the barren earth that surrounded it, waiting to claim it completely. A Mexican woman drove a wagon with sacks of rice and flour, said to be for the lady Mrs. Luft. The Indians speculated that she worked in Santa Rosa for wealthy friends of the Lufts, but since they dared not follow the wagon, never traveling farther west than Sebastopol, they weren't certain that the supplies were even for Mrs. Luft. How does she live? they wondered. What does she eat? But then, as it turned out, it was the same Mexican woman who let the mortician and the sheriff into the house. And it was the sheriff who described for the newspapers the great room full of flowers and vegetables growing in pots beneath the large new windows, and Mrs. Luft, dressed as if ready for her funeral, was laid out on a single bed amidst the blooms.

The Indians laughed among themselves, hiding from one another whatever trepidation they may have felt. "She listened to

Kaloopis," they joked. "Can't you see her going about that room smelling flowers?"

Years later, when there wasn't a trace of the magnificent house. Passersby would see nothing other than an expanse of lifeless earth, but the older Indians gathered and told stories about the old woman who had once lived there and then become a legend. As for Catfish, he died shortly after he and his stout wife left Luft Rancheria. She continued to boast about his bravery, forever reminding people of his journey through the woods to find Kaloopis. The people always wondered whether that was what had angered Kaloopis. Or was it only after they banned him from their children that he set his curse upon the land? The expert seamstress reminded them that she had talked to Mrs. Luft about his curse.

"That's when she banished *me* from the house," she said.

They wondered if Mrs. Luft ever believed the expert seamstress or, for that matter, ever considered the possibility that she, Mrs. Luft herself, might be under a spell.

But it didn't matter what she believed or didn't believe. Looking out her window the day the expert seamstress spoke to her, and in the days and weeks ahead, she saw what any of them could have seen: Kaloopis's curse was his absence.

Part Nine

Question Woman sat puzzled. "How did the story about a man who learned to smell flowers make a *good* story for anyone? That man Catfish didn't really learn what he needed to. And in the end the lady Mrs. Luft died."

"Sister, Catfish didn't learn. But the lady Mrs. Luft listened to Kaloopis and knew to take care of the flowers. She died—they both died, Catfish and Mrs. Luft—but the story remains."

"Mrs. Luft wasn't an Indian," Question Woman said, still thinking about the story.

"True," answered Answer Woman. "Her people wandered far from the Mountain. Indians just below the Mountain here didn't go as far. But no matter what history, how far from the Mountain we wandered, we risk forgetting the stories. It's what makes people human beings."

"You've said that before," quipped Question Woman.

"Ha! In case you forgot!"

"Ha yourself. In case *you* forgot so that you would have to tell me again."

"I thought you might question how the hummingbird in the story about Isabel was a woman but here, in that last story, Hummingbird was a man."

"I can figure that out," said Question Woman. "Each has the

spirit of Hummingbird, which, man or woman, connects them to the ancient stories of the Mountain and all of creation."

"I guess you won't be asking questions anymore. You're so smart."

"Ha ha!"

The two sisters sat awhile. A car passed on the road, and then another, people returning home from work.

"It's getting late. We should go soon," said Answer Woman. "Remember, we can't see well in the dark."

"I'm still stuck on the lady Mrs. Luft. I don't like that she died."

"She died in the story, but not in the life of the story," answered Answer Woman. "And that way she doesn't die. She lives."

"That's confusing."

"Look, Sister, unless we forget the stories, they continue to live, as do the people in them. It's all we've got to pass from one generation to the next. Think of a seed. It has inside its shell all of the information a plant needs to grow. It knows what food it must have from the earth. It knows to grow toward the sun. We aren't born with the information in us like that. We've got stories. They must live if we are to live."

"I think I get it," said Question Woman, and then a moment later she said, "So, tell a story about a story being timeless."

"Every story I tell does that. But I think I know what you mean. But remember, it's getting late."

"What's the story?"

"It's about a girl who sees a giant sturgeon. Listen."

A Girl Sees a Giant Sturgeon

here was much rain. Creeks overflowed. The lagoon spread from Sebastopol to the sea. Near the town of Novato, where the marshy wetlands crossed the freeway, the girl stood on a hillside watching the dark form in the water that had come to greet her.

It was ten feet long. The girl was ten. It was more than twice her length. Its prickly dorsal fin showed above the water, which was how she was able to trace its movement as it drew closer and closer, before it stopped in water shallow enough for her to see her reflection in each of its round, black eyes.

"My poor daughter, now she has seen a fish," exclaimed Alice to a neighbor, exasperated.

The neighbor, a lonely busybody, was anxious to entertain Alice's confidences, especially about the girl. The girl's mother was not Alice but, rather, a cousin of Alice's who had fallen on hard times, too many children and too little money, leaving the girl with Alice and then disappearing altogether, but not before making adoption arrangements. "You have no children, no man," she told Alice. "The girl will be good for you. She is the most unusual of my children. She has a great imagination. She sees things." It was the late 1960s. San Francisco, a half hour south of

Novato, was the home of hippie culture. Alice was not a hippie, but her cousin pitched imagination and visions as if these attributes would make having the girl a bargain.

Alice was a schoolteacher. She was forty and, yes, single. One long-term boyfriend and then another had been enough, at least for now. Why not adopt the girl? She did everything right. She made certain her daughter had the healthiest foods. She talked her through homework. She gave her daughter her own bedroom, her private living space, and together they decorated it with bright colors. She'd grown to love her, so accustomed to the routine of cooking and caring for her that she could no longer imagine life without her.

Yet she felt as if something were missing: her inability to understand the source of the girl's wild stories, something she interpreted as a failure for someone calling herself a mother. Nevertheless, she entertained her daughter's stories. And she learned not to question her daughter's strange or inappropriate answers to questions, no matter how curious she was or how disturbed about them she might be. But the stories, detailed, often outlandish, frightened Alice. What was she to do with them? How was she to respond?

Complicating matters were the girl's sudden bursts of rage, something Alice's cousin hadn't mentioned. What prompted the anger? Something as simple as not being able to find her hairbrush or a lost crayon. Alice was not familiar with younger children (Alice taught high school), but a counselor told Alice the child was using her imagination to transcend trauma, that it was a behavior learned before her life with Alice. The outbursts of anger, the same. Time and a stable environment would be the solution. That her daughter didn't make friends seemed to concern Alice more than her daughter, though Alice constantly reassured her that she was special and that her classmates had no reason not to like her. Still, Alice felt there was something more she needed to know, and her conversations with the neighbor, if they didn't solve Alice's anxiety, at least alleviated the loneliness and sense of despair that accompanied it.

"So, what must I do?" Alice continued with the neighbor.

"What you've done before," the neighbor answered. "Like when she was seeing the so-called little people or talking to a bird. Listen to her. Don't tell her those things aren't real. Just listen and maybe you'll see a pattern and learn something. But Alice, for God's sake, don't let her go close to those floodwaters alone. It's dangerous."

Alice told herself that her daughter had merely gone down the street, to the end of the cul-de-sac, where she could see the rising water from safely atop the hill. Nonetheless, after her conversation with the neighbor, she went to look for her daughter, only to discover that she was indeed close to the water. But it wasn't the water that caused her to gasp and then scream for her daughter to step back. Out of the water, no more than three feet from the girl, was the enormous black head of the fish, as still as a rock.

It was huge. With its large head, she thought of a whale, even though with its gaping mouth and gills opening and closing like doors, she could see otherwise. Hardly could she think but to grab the girl and pull her to safety. Clutching her daughter's arm, she stood taking in the sight of this giant creature half submerged in water, and then quickly walked her daughter home.

"How long were you standing there?" she asked her daughter.

"Forever," her daughter answered.

As Alice prepared dinner, stuffing two skinned chicken breasts into the oven, she attempted to recreate in her mind what had happened. There were dark clouds, weren't there? Past the fish was murky water covering the freeway, clear to the San Francisco Bay beyond. An endless sea. Did she see the expanse of water, or was she just remembering newspaper pictures of the flood? She couldn't tell. The water seemed as unreal as the half-submerged fish. She could not make sense of things. That she had seen the fish with her daughter, and that she knew her daughter had stood alongside the fish before, called up the nagging feeling she'd had that she'd been an inadequate mother, that there was something about her daughter she couldn't reach. Certainly, as the neighbor suggested, she'd been irresponsible. Her daughter did not talk about the fish that night, and neither did Alice.

"Have you heard something about fish washing up after these rains?" she asked her neighbor on the phone the next day.

"Aren't you teaching?" the neighbor asked, surprised to hear from Alice in the middle of the day.

"Yes, but was it in the newspaper?"

"What?"

"Something about a fish." Alice began to feel already that she'd said too much. "I'm on my lunch break."

Then the neighbor said, "What, dead fish? All the more reason to keep your daughter in the house. Salmonella."

The fish did not go away. Each afternoon, Alice followed her
daughter to the water. She felt a confrontation with her daughter
would come to pass if she forbade her to see the fish. As much as
the sight of the enormous sea creature unnerved her, she needed
to protect her daughter. She scoured newspapers, listened to the
news, but nowhere was there mention of the fish. Hadn't neighbors walking their dogs past the cul-de-sac seen it? She no longer broached the subject with her busybody neighbor. She felt
embarrassed, not only because of the possibility the fish wasn't
real but because, for whatever reason, maybe it was there only for
her and her daughter to see. Which was why she never called the
Fish and Game Agency.

The rain never stopped. Two weeks passed. The waters drew
back, across the freeway to the bay. Water-soaked tree trunks and
rock outcroppings could be seen above the still-murky waters
that covered the wetlands. Days passed as they had before the
fish, with Alice's daughter retreating to her room, telling herself
stories or blankly staring out the window rather than doing her
homework, until Alice called her to dinner.

Then one day she didn't come home. It was the police who
found her, and the school principal who informed a panicked
Alice that her daughter had taken the wrong bus home. But Alice
knew otherwise. When Alice came to retrieve her daughter, she
saw her below the railroad tracks that paralleled the freeway. She
was ankle-deep in mud and reeds with the fish.

The policeman who was there saw the fish, and in fact several police officers who had showed up that afternoon saw the fish. The school principal saw it. What a coincidence this lost child found herself next to this enormous fish, they said. But for Alice it was no coincidence. The next day, photographers, newspaper reporters, and a TV news crew swarmed the fish. The Fish and Game Agency identified the fish as a sturgeon, yes, unusually large and no doubt quite old. They assured the gathering crowds that it was not dangerous, just as they had when first called by the police. They figured that it was lost, speculation corroborated by a local historian, who reminded the curious onlookers that before the freeway had been built and the wetlands diked, it was not unusual to spot large sturgeon swimming in the shallow waters.

"You didn't say it was alive," the busybody neighbor complained to Alice.

They were seated in Alice's kitchen, safe from the press or neighbors Alice imagined might approach the house to talk to the girl who'd first seen the fish. Alice had pulled the curtains over the front room windows that faced the street. Now, with her neighbor in the kitchen light, she felt intruded upon, felt a need to protect her daughter and herself.

"It's huge. Its head is out of the water," she told the busybody neighbor, only reciting the obvious. "I wonder if it will find its way back from wherever it came," she let out.

Over the days that followed, more and more people came to see the fish. They told stories about its origins. Songs were sung, offerings made. Occasionally, it slipped back underwater, only to resurface minutes later, dashing hopes that it might find its way back to sea. Hippies claimed it signaled the dawn of the Age of Aquarius. A Catholic priest doused it with holy water. Monks chanted, seeing in its large, still head and rhythmically gaping mouth and gills a perfect manifestation of Buddha consciousness. Developers, anxious to dike more of the wetlands, saw it as a nuisance.

The Indians had their own stories. There were several about a woman who had sat so long by the water that she had turned to stone. A Coast Miwok woman whose great-grandmother had lived on the old rancheria in nearby Nicasio pointed to a rock near the water and said that was the woman. A Coast Miwok man from Petaluma, farther north, agreed, adding that the woman had gotten stuck there the last time the seas rose, when people had to seek higher ground, though he could not confirm which of the rocks near the water she had become. It was a Southern Pomo woman from Sebastopol who told of a sturgeon. "That fish is from the ancient times on Sonoma Mountain when the animals were still people," she said. "That woman sitting there who turned to stone, she thought the fish was looking for Sonoma Mountain, which was many miles away. Maybe she thought if it came out of the water, if she waited long enough, she would find it turned into a handsome man. Ha! If it was a handsome man, she wasn't going to show him the way home, and that's why she got punished."

Alice, sitting with her daughter among the crowds, took

comfort in the distraction of the raucous debates and the singing and chanting that surrounded her. When a newspaper writer
or one or another of the onlookers invaded her and her daughter's reverie to ask questions, she merely said to them what she
herself wanted to believe, which was that, like everyone else, she
and her daughter were just watching the fish. But alone at night
she could not fool herself. She felt a thickening wall of darkness
surrounding her and separating her from her daughter, such that
she found herself making silly mistakes, dropping utensils as she
prepared dinner, but then, at least for a moment, she was able to
pull herself together, wade into that darkness, and push through
it to find her daughter. Even if it didn't change things, she was
able to prove to herself that it was possible to reach the girl inside
that shadow world.

Still, though, she couldn't focus on her lesson plans. She
couldn't grade papers. After many days and nights of feeling this
way, she found she was often rushing down the hallway to her
daughter's bedroom, both during the day and in the middle of
the night. "Do you need help with your homework?" she'd ask.
"Did you hear a noise outside?" Her daughter, either staring out
her window in the afternoon or awakened in her bed at night,
never answered her, leaving Alice standing there feeling stupid
and alone.

Spring arrived. Daffodils in the gardens. New growth on the
trees. The marsh waters continued to roll back, and with them
the sturgeon. Alice and her daughter followed. The crowds had
lessened, as some people, while wishing the creature a safe return

to the sea, had lost patience and others had simply lost interest. Still, Alice and her daughter never found themselves alone, as they were surrounded often by travelers from afar who had heard of the fish as a local attraction. Their presence was why Alice managed to contain her initial reaction when, one afternoon while seated with her daughter on a log deeper into the marsh's reeds, she saw herself reflected in the fish's eyes. The sight had caught her off guard, but she quickly looked away, hoping no one else had seen the interaction. But then she made the mistake of looking a second time. Only then, seeing how clearly she was framed in those fathomless dark orbs, did she gasp. She looked for her daughter in the reflection and found her seated next to her, just as she was on the log.

"Do you see how the fish sees us?" she whispered. The girl turned to Alice as if perplexed by the question. "Can you see yourself in the sturgeon's eyes?" Alice asked then, to which the girl, whispering, answered plainly but with an impish smile, "Yes."

Alice did not want to believe what she had thought after she'd first seen the fish all those days ago: that it was somehow there for her and her daughter. Even now she tried to dismiss the haunted feeling she had after seeing her reflection in the fish's eyes. It was only a reflection from the spring afternoon's bright sun, she told herself. And yet, why hadn't she seen it before? She tried to joke, saying to herself, It's not Jonah in a whale's stomach but poor Alice in a sturgeon's eyes. But nothing worked to shake her odd feeling. From then on, she saw herself in the darkness that surrounded her each night, just as she'd seen herself in the reflection. And her daughter wouldn't let her forget. Little did Alice know how the impish smile her daughter had shown that afternoon foretold of things to come.

Her daughter became uncontrollable. She reveled in her bad behavior, taunting Alice first with her impish smile every time Alice said anything to her, then with outright acts of disobedience. Certainly, her daughter had been obstinate in the past and displayed sudden outbursts of anger, but never had she streaked the walls with her crayons or tossed pots and pans across the kitchen, and for no other reason than that it seemed to get Alice's attention.

At night, the girl began opening her bedroom window, as if telling Alice she was going to run away. Alice nailed the window shut and then slept, if you could call it sleeping, in a chair in front of her daughter's bedroom door, lest she try to escape through the front of the house. Alice tried to reason with her, which did little more than encourage greater disobedience. The girl wouldn't go to school, and Alice wrote one excuse after another. "Don't I take you to see the fish every day?" she asked her daughter. "What more do you want me to do?" But these questions, the same as with anything else Alice might say to her, were met only with that impish smile.

Alice didn't want to talk about the fish. Talking about it only solidified the darkness pulling Alice deeper and deeper into its depths. Alice could not extricate the appearance of the enormous sea creature from all that was happening with her daughter.

Seated in the dark at night, she remembered her daughter's eyes, open and vulnerable, when she'd first met her. The little girl seemed unusually alive. Alice always had that nagging sense that she needed to do more to reach the girl, but now, losing control each time her daughter approached the bedroom door as if to escape in the middle of the night, Alice couldn't help but scream, "What do you want? What do you want me to do?"

Her daughter began acting out in public. One afternoon while watching the fish, she bolted up from the log and raced toward the busy freeway. More than once she waded deep enough into the muddy marsh and then began swimming into the open sea. She spat at the onlookers. All of the madness Alice lived with at home was now out in the open for all to see.

When Alice's busybody neighbor said, "She's unbalanced," Alice thought to herself, No more so than me.

Alice had no choice but to return to the counselor. "It's post trauma," the counselor told Alice. "You've had her for enough time now, what, a year or so? As she settles in with you her past will come up. If it, her bad behavior, doesn't stop, we could give her medication."

But that's what worried Alice, that the girl's behavior wouldn't stop. Medication, but then what? How long could she say to herself and others, "I'm getting counseling," if nothing changed? The thought of punishing her daughter by keeping her from the fish frightened Alice, as if doing so would open a hole of darkness she would never find her way out of. Wasn't she face-to-face with losing her daughter?

A hippie gave Alice a stick of lit incense to hold. A monk meditated. The priest suggested an exorcism. "I can't watch this anymore," the busybody neighbor told Alice. "Something's missing with that girl. She isn't right."

The Indians had their theories. One was that Alice's daughter was possessed by an ancient evil spirit. Another was that her daughter's behavior was a punishment upon all people for what the white man had done to the old sturgeon's home. Wasn't that what the sturgeon was saying, that the wetlands had been destroyed?

It was with a group of Indians that Alice first saw the tall woman. She had stepped out from between two men.

She was so solid and square beneath her billowing dress that she gave Alice the impression of a rock sprung up from the earth below her. She wore a scarf over her head that was the blue color of the water beyond the reeds.

"She is going to sing a song," one of the two men said, stepping forward alongside her.

"For the sturgeon to return home," said the other man, coming forward then.

It was late afternoon. A cool breeze blew seaward. The woman was an Indian, which Alice understood not so much by her complexion as by the talk she overheard from among the other Indians. The woman was neither Coast Miwok nor Southern Pomo but from a tribe farther north on the coast.

"What's she going to do, communicate with the fish?" asked a hippie.

"She might be connecting her spirit to it," offered a woman with a dog on a leash.

The tall woman raised her arms toward the giant fish and began singing. She sang for the longest time, a repetitive chant that wafted over the crowd with the effect of a lullaby. When she finished, dropping her arms to her side, she stood looking at the giant sea creature. It began sliding in and out of the water, its gaping mouth and gills rapidly opening and closing, as if awakened by the song rather than lulled to sleep. Still, it did not leave the shore.

"What was that song supposed to do?" asked a young man wearing a T-shirt and baseball cap.

"Send the fish home," the two Indian men standing alongside the tall woman answered in unison.

"How long is it going to take before it leaves?" the young man asked then. Clearly, he was skeptical, attempting to bait the tall woman and her two friends.

It was then that Alice's busybody neighbor spoke up, addressing the tall woman. "What about the girl?" she asked, pointing to Alice's daughter. "What can you do to help her?"

"The mother will have to do that," the tall woman answered.

Alice shuddered, not just because there was no doubt that the neighbor had all along seen her as a failure as a mother, but now the entire crowd was thinking it too. It was as if she'd been convicted in a court of law.

That night, Alice took the chair she'd been sitting in and moved it next to her daughter's bed. There was something her daughter needed, and because Alice couldn't understand what it was, she'd always felt a distance from her, and the giant fish beached in the floodwaters had only made the distance more obvious. Alice felt blind. She reached in the dark for her daughter's hand, her only assurance that she had not already lost her.

Days turned into nights. Little by little, the sturgeon moved out to sea, farther and farther, until only its jagged black dorsal fin could be seen above the water. Some people claimed that the tall Indian woman's song had finally worked. Others said the receded waters and a regular tide helped the giant fish navigate its way back to the sea. Alice, fearing the crowds, stayed at home and kept her arms around her daughter. She felt as if she were in a dream. She lost track of time, even as she cooked and cleaned and wrote one excuse and then another for why her daughter was not in school. She no longer heard what people were saying or paid attention to anything beyond her daughter, which was why when she found that the fish was gone, she was so surprised.

One day she was seated on a rock. It was early morning. Beyond the reeds the sun was a golden road across the water. Alice felt the cool air and figured a fog had lifted. She could see. Realizing the fish was gone, she thought of her daughter and panicked. But she was there next to her, safe. And she wasn't struggling. She was awake and calm. Alice then felt the warmth of the sun's reflection reach her. No one had come yet to look for the fish; she and her daughter were alone. Looking at the girl under her arm, Alice had a picture of all she needed to know. The fish hadn't caused what Alice couldn't understand and what her daughter didn't know how to ask for. Whatever the case, whether it was the fish finding her daughter, or her daughter finding it, the giant sturgeon had brought them to this moment. How long otherwise would it have taken Alice to know her daughter needed her mother's arms to hold her? She loved her daughter, she always had, but she hadn't raised the child in the first years of her life, and she herself hadn't had enough experience to know what the girl needed. She thought how she might explain this to others. She thought of telling some story about the sturgeon. But her daughter, as if confirming what Alice understood, nestled closer to her, and all Alice could say was, "Remember the fish."

The fish never returned. People talked for a while, told stories, and then eventually the giant sturgeon seemed altogether to be forgotten. Developers diked more of the wetlands. The Indians, finding themselves lost in the marshes, argued among themselves over which outcropping of rocks had been a woman turned to stone, or whether a bulldozer had carried it away.

Alice and her daughter always found a place to sit by the water. Alice never did come out and say what it was she'd come to understand, and neither did either of them remember the difficult times before the fish. They did, however, endeavor to learn everything they could about the life of a sturgeon. Seated together, picture books and encyclopedias open on their laps, they talked on and on, always with the thought that in the wide open sea before them a giant sturgeon might be swimming. They knew the Indian stories and, like the Indians, debated between themselves which rock had been a woman turned to stone and whether or not it had something to do with a sturgeon.

Sometimes one would talk more than the other. In the years

ahead, if her daughter stressed over a college exam or suffered a broken romance, Alice knew it would comfort the girl to recite everything they knew about the giant fish. Years later still, when Alice could no longer find her keys or remember the day of the week, her daughter knew she didn't need to talk at all. It was enough to keep her arm around her mother.

Part Ten

"I like that story about the girl who sees a giant sturgeon," said Question Woman.

"What did you say?" asked Answer Woman.

"Aren't you listening to me?"

Answer Woman, looking out over the valley, turned back to her sister.

"Aren't you listening to me?" Question Woman repeated, annoyed.

"Yes, Sister, I hear you. You liked the story about the girl who sees a giant sturgeon."

"Yes."

"What did you like about it?"

"It was happy at the end. And I understood what you were saying before, how the story, any story, lives on."

Question Woman, sensing that her sister was still distracted, said again, "Are you listing to me?"

"Yes, I'm listening," answered Answer Woman, and then to prove herself added, "The story lives on even as it changes, even as the lives of the characters reliving the stories come and go."

"I'm kind of getting it, I think. We keep reliving the stories because we keep forgetting the things they have to tell us." Question Woman took a deep breath then, still convinced Answer

Woman was not giving her her full attention. "Are you listening to me? Of all things, I have answers for once in my life and you are not paying attention to me. Oh, and don't get smart and tell me that if I have answers you don't need to tell stories. I can figure that out too."

"Okay. I'll admit, my mind is on something else," said Answer Woman. "Look," she said, gesturing with an outstretched wing to the valley. "The fog is coming over the western hills. It is getting late. Soon it will be dark and we need to get home. Are you so smart now that you've forgotten we can't see in the dark?"

"Oh, please, just one more story," begged Question Woman. "Ha! Just think how many more answers I might have, how much more in this world I'll understand, with just one more story. Oh, and I won't bother you all day tomorrow with questions, I promise."

"I'll believe that when I see it."

"Sister, now you are being mean. Please, just one more story. Make it about time again, how the stories last."

"Okay, I have one about a time we might not have seen yet: the future."

"What? That's confusing," said Question Woman.

"Listen, it's the last story for the day."

"What is it?"

"It's about the people on Sonoma Mountain having a storytelling contest."

"In the future?"

"Listen."

The People on Sonoma Mountain Have a Storytelling Contest

They ate fish. Sometimes, if they were lucky, they found eggs. The mountain was a desert. Rocks and sage scrub. Recently, colorful fish appeared in the warm ocean water that surrounded the mountain, and sailfish too. And because of the large sword-beaked sailfish that they could spear and the colorful fish they could draw in nets, people for the first time in memory had plenty to eat, which was no doubt why they had time to ponder faraway lands.

Across the wide sea they could see three mountaintops. They had stories about each. The mountain to the north was Helena. It was a name passed down from people who lived on the land below Sonoma Mountain before the waters rose. And as with the sharp peak to the west called Tamalpais, no one could agree on who or what the names meant, even as they told stories about them. Only for Diablo, the mountain peak to the south, could they remember and understand what the name meant, *diablo* being a word for the devil. On their own story they agreed: When the waters rose, Sonoma Mountain called the good people home.

There were two villages, one on the west side of the mountain, the other on the east. Between them, below the mountain's peak, was a long gorge that in recent years filled with water each winter before it dried in summer. Ducks and geese, in ever greater numbers, nested along its banks, the birds and their eggs, like the plentiful fish in the sea, providing the people more time to think and wonder. A headwoman from each village formed a court that settled conflicts should disagreements arise between the two villages. The woman representing the east village had to be elected by citizens from the west village, and vice versa. Both had to be skilled in the art of consensus, such that no decision on any disagreement could be arrived at without consensus from both villages. After some time, when talk of travel to a distant mountain peak turned to which of the two villages would send representatives out to sea first, the two women said there should be a storytelling contest. The village that told the best story would send its representatives upon the water, and they would carry the story to the new land.

The people of both villages agreed.

It was decided that the contest winners would go to Tamalpais. Helena, to the north, would be too difficult, for there was the ever-present possibility that a strong flow tide could carry their small boats forever past Helena's peak. Stories persisted about Diablo's violent winds and who knew what else associated with its name. But, gauging the tides correctly, they'd long fished in waters halfway to Tamalpais and returned safely.

"You must now go back to your village and together with your villagers find the best story to tell should you meet people on Tamalpais," said the headwoman of the western village.

"And we will meet at the gorge, halfway between our two

villages," said the headwoman of the eastern village. "It is mid-day. We will meet here the same time tomorrow. We will hear the stories and decide which one is best."

Both women were elderly, boundless in spirit and wisdom. They served for many years, fulfilling their duty to achieve consensus whenever disagreement arose between the villages, but also working together should there be a conflict between citizens within the same village. Each knew the citizens of both villages well. The western village, the largest of the two, had the best view of Tamalpais. Its citizens, most familiar with the tides, considered themselves the best fishermen. The easterners, upon whom the western villagers depended for the best chaparral for their seagoing boats, fancied themselves the best hunters, with both ducks and geese nesting along the gorge, plus iguanas on the rocky cliffs being more plentiful on their side of the mountain.

It was said that the two women sometimes disagreed. They might have differences of opinion, in which case they would retreat to a special place on the mountain known only to them. Some said it was a small house below the cliffs. Others said it was a cave in the cliffs, and still others said it was merely a quiet place among the thick chaparral. What was certain was that, wherever it was they met, they traded stories, asked questions, and conversed with the ancient spirits of the mountain, who could summon any story ever told. Which was why when the usually prompt headwomen showed up late the next day, the villagers figured they'd lost track of time talking about the contest.

The villagers were lined up: the easterners on the east side of the gorge, the westerners on the west. The two headwomen, laughing out loud at the villagers, stood at the north end of the gorge, where it ended in an open track of sand.

"How are you going to hear each other's stories standing so far from one another?" the headwoman of the east village shouted.

"Come here together," the headwoman of the west village called out.

Embarrassed, and grumbling about having to collect together in a contest, the villagers joined the two headwomen.

"You don't want to hear each other's stories?" questioned the headwoman of the east village.

"How are you going to know which story is best and that the contest is fair?" added the headwoman of the west village.

Iguana Eye, a leader from the east village and the person chosen to tell its story, stepped forward. Some said he got his name for his black, shiny eyes, others said that the name was on account of his sand-colored skin. He was a small, lithe man, an expert orator, and he had such a quick smile that when he answered the eastern headwoman, "Yes, you are right. We know you are fair," not too few of the western villagers figured he was attempting to win her favor.

"We will see which village goes first," said the headwoman of the east.

The headwoman of the west handed her the gambling stick, a flattened chaparral branch with a rattlesnake carving on one side symbolizing the hunters of the east, and on the other side a fish for the fishermen of the west. Together, the headwomen tossed the stick into the air. The villagers drew close and watched as the stick landed on the ground between them, showing the rattlesnake.

"Oh," said Iguana Eye. "And just think if we hadn't come together here, we wouldn't be seeing for ourselves who won."

"I thought you just said our headwomen are fair. Don't you trust them?" quipped Orange Sunfish, the leader and orator for the west, his name associated with his curly orange hair.

"Enough," said the headwoman of the west village.

Iguana Eye stepped forward. He took a deep breath, stretched his arms over his head.

"So, this is what happened," he began:

There were so many people the earth began to sink. They no longer saw the animals and birds, they didn't see plants or trees. They had long forgot the stories of this wonderous mountain. They saw nothing but their own creations, tall buildings, houses made of shiny rocks. And knowing nothing but themselves and their creations, they forgot that all the animals and birds and plants and trees were people like themselves. And even though there were so many of these people, they felt alone, separate from one another. Which was why they made taller and taller buildings to protect themselves from other villages, and thicker and thicker walls to protect themselves even from one another in the same village. This was the curse they suffered once they forgot the mountain's stories, once they forgot that they were kin to all of life.

As the water began to flood their villages, as the angry earth no longer wanted to carry the weight of these people, they began to fight over villages on the highest hills and then over the highest rooms in the tall buildings. They were killing one another. People were drowning. There was less food to eat. Soon there would be no one left.

That's when a lone woman in a boat found herself adrift in an enemy village. She saw someone paddling a boat, a silhouette in the distance, and when this person began calling for her to stop, she panicked, thinking it was an enemy villager coming to arrest or murder her. Perhaps it was the tide against her or her pure panic, but she found she could not move her boat. As it turned out, she saw that the approaching figure was a woman much like herself, elderly, and then she was no longer afraid. She wondered if the woman might've been lost somehow within her own territory. Clearly, the woman belonged to the enemy village. She wore the earrings and the green-and-yellow-striped face paint of its villagers.

"Please forgive me," she said to the woman. "The tide has carried me into your water."

"The water belongs to everyone," the woman from the enemy village said.

"Nobody believes that," answered the first woman.

"That's why, unless we do something different, we will all die soon."

As they talked, they discovered that their boats had drifted into open water beyond the villages, and they could see the peak of a mountain in the distance.

"That must be the enchanted land people once talked about, where humans spoke to animals and lived peacefully," said the woman from the enemy village.

The longer they drifted upon the open sea, the more they talked of the ancient mountain and found themselves telling stories they'd either forgotten or couldn't remember hearing.

"The mountain is speaking to us," said the first woman.

"Yes," agreed the enemy villager. "We must go there."

"First, we must try to get back to our villages and tell what we have learned," said the first woman.

"All right, but we must be careful, for our own people could kill us, not trusting what we are telling them. After all, we come from warring villages."

The two women were very careful whom they talked to. When they met on the open sea, each had only ten people who followed them. And that way, they came to Sonoma Mountain. Since the mountain was so bare of food, they decided that one group would go to the east side of the mountain and the other to the west.

"Wait," said the woman of the first village. "We could start a war with one another if we forget the lessons of our enemy villages."

"I know what we'll do," answered the woman from the other village. "We will trade places. You go with my people and I will go with yours."

Iguana Eye, finishing his story, bowed politely and addressed the women.

"So, my honorable judges, that is the story my people want to tell. It explains why to this day we elect women from the west to lead people in the east and vice versa. And why you headwomen are so necessary to our survival. The stories are passed down from these headwomen before you. That is how we remember the stories and honor your gift. How else would we remember and tell the stories you know and tell?"

"Very good," said the headwoman of the east and the headwoman of the west in unison.

Orange Sunfish, the storyteller for the west, then stepped forward. He took a deep breath, stretched his arms over his head.

"The story I am going to tell is quite amazing, if I may say so myself. Listen:

There weren't two villages. There was one. And it was so big it covered more than half the earth. What was left was planted in food for the people. They grew food that the animals and birds would not eat. They could stick these plants in the ground and make them grow, just as we can pull a reed out of mud here at the gorge in one place and watch it grow in another place until summer turns the gorge to desert again. Which is what began to happen in the story I am telling. The water, lonesome for the animals and birds, began to disappear. It was tired of feeding just the giant village and its plants. After all, it is water's nature to share.

As you might expect, people began to fight. People were limited to no more than a handful of water each day. That's all they had to drink. And without the water, there was less food.

The water continued to disappear, people not understanding it was a warning. But at this point, what could people do? The old storytellers had been warning people for a long time to remember the animals and the birds. They knew that the water wanted to share. Once the animals and birds were gone, no one knew how to get them back. Soon, generations were born who knew only of the animals and birds in stories.

The people tried different ways to get the water back, to stop the earth from drying. They talked to the clouds, but the clouds would not answer. They talked to the dry streams and gorges, but the water would not rise. The water would not talk back. They tried to trick the water, planting carvings of birds and animals in places the water once lived, but the water would not be fooled.

The people of this giant village became more restless. They became frightened. Fearing they would die of thirst, they began to steal water from one another. Yes, one handful at a time. But what happened? They spilled what water was left and became more thirsty and restless than before. That was when a man rose up at one end of this giant village and said, "There is not enough water for everyone. We must get rid of people on the other side of the village," and the people on his side of the village agreed.

But it was one village, no matter how large it was. Word traveled to the other end of the village. A man rose up there and told the villagers on his side of the village that they must be prepared to defend themselves.

Both men created large war parties, the war party from one end of the village preparing to attack, the other readying itself

for the attack. When a fire broke out at one end of the village,
the villagers there believed the war party from the opposite end
of the village had set the fire. "They are going to burn us down,"
claimed the man who had risen up as the leader on that side of
the village. He instructed his warriors to set fire to the other
end of the village, and the warriors at the other end retaliated,
setting more fires. Soon the entire village was on fire. Dark
clouds covered the earth. There was no water to put the fire out.

Those who could escape began to run. They headed to the
fields where food grew, but even there the vines and stalks
were on fire. There was nothing to eat. Only a few people got
far enough away that they once again could see the light of day
beyond the clouds of smoke. That's when they saw a mountain
in the distance. And they could see it was not on fire.

They ran toward the mountain. Once they found themselves
below its steep, dry hills, they stopped to rest. Behind them the
entire earth was enshrouded in black smoke.

It was the leaders from each end of the village who found
themselves and a few of their survivors collected together.
Though they had escaped the destruction they had created,
already they began to fight, arguing which group of villagers
would travel up to the mountain and live, since it appeared the
dry mountain would not provide much food, let alone enough
water for everyone.

Then, a woman from each side stepped forward and offered
a solution. Both women were elderly. They spoke taking turns,
saying, "Have you not listened to the mountain that has called

us here? There is a solution. One group of us will go to the east side of the mountain and one will go to the west. There will be enough food and water as long as we remember not to repeat the bad behavior that got us here. You must respect and listen to the mountain. It has saved us.

The people of both sides agreed. They saw that these two women could hear the mountain. They knew these two women could tell the mountain's stories, reminding them to live right and peaceful. And that's when, as one group began to head east and the other west, the women spoke again: "We will trade places, each going with the other's people. And that's the way it will be from now on."

The mountain provided enough food and water for everyone. Over time the dark clouds covering the earth vanished and oceans filled the land.

Orange Sunfish, his story complete, took a deep breath, again stretched his arms.

"Honorable headwomen," he said, "that is our story, the people of the west. You who talk to birds, you who are elected because you are worthy to hear the Mountain's stories, you who know the secrets of the animals, we hope you find our story worthy."

Iguana Eye came forth then. "Honorable headwomen," he said, "you who we elect from one village to serve the other village. You, our honorable headwoman of the east, we elected you from the western village because it was clear that you could hear the Mountain's stories and serve our village well. We have done our best to honor you and make our home your home. And you, most honorable headwoman of the west, you are our kin, you hail from the eastern village, don't forget. We never had any doubt that the westerners would choose you as their headwoman for, like your counterpart among us, you can hear and tell the Mountain's stories."

The two headwomen nodded appreciatively to Orange Sunfish and Iguana Eye and to both groups of villagers.

"Now, which story will be the winner?" asked Orange Sunfish.

The two women chuckled at Orange Sunfish's anxiousness.

"Certainly, you must see which story is the best," Iguana Eye quickly rejoined.

The two headwomen chuckled again.

"What if we say it is a tie?" said the headwoman of the eastern village.

"Well, that can't be. There is clearly a winner," said Iguana Eye.

"Yes, it is quite clear that there is a winner," said Orange Sunfish. "It is most obvious to anyone who has heard the stories."

"Well, it is a tie," said the headwomen in unison. "Both stories are equally good. They teach the same lesson: We must not forget the stories."

The villagers grumbled, clearly dissatisfied, but not nearly as much as their designated storytellers, Orange Sunfish and Iguana Eye.

"So does that mean both villages send people to Tamalpais?" asked Iguana Eye.

"Yes, why not?" agreed Orange Sunfish. "We both have strong oarsmen who could stem the tides in our boats."

"It is not enough to be strong," the headwoman of the western village told Orange Sunfish.

"And what if you are attacked upon arrival, should you encounter hostile villagers at Tamalpais?" asked the headwoman of the eastern village.

"We will return safely," answered Iguana Eye, stepping closer to the two women. "You honorable headwomen, you teach peace. We will honor your teaching and not engage in war. We will honor the lessons in the stories we told. They are, as you have said, equally good."

"And what if you are captured?" asked the headwoman of the western village, looking directly at Iguana Eye.

Before Iguana Eye could answer, Orange Sunfish stepped forward and said, "We will do our best to stay alive. We are brave no matter which village we come from."

"It is not enough to be brave," the headwoman of the eastern village told him.

"Then what must we do?" Orange Sunfish asked.

A chorus of children from both villages shouted, "Tell the captors' stories! Tell more stories!"

The headwomen laughed with joy. "Yes!" they said.

The children continued to shout, "Tell more stories! Tell more stories!"

When at last the children quieted, the headwoman of the western village said, "We have heard only two stories. How are we going to know who has the *best* stories, not just *one* good story?"

"Sister," the headwoman of the eastern village addressed the headwoman of the western village. "You have a question, but isn't the answer clear? The contest must go on."

One story after another was told, back and forth between Iguana Eye and Orange Sunfish. The headwomen and the villagers heard a story from long before water covered the earth below the Mountain, when a million people stopped having children until only a few people were left. The Mountain beckoned those few remaining people, and they found life again and had children. Another story told of insects poisoning people, a plague upon the earth, at which time two women with a song to stop the insects led the survivors to the Mountain after they heard its call.

As each storyteller continued, the villagers heard stories they couldn't remember hearing before. One story opened up the door to another story. It was as if the headwomen had let loose the stories from wherever it was on the Mountain they gathered secretly to hear them. Iguana Eye and Orange Sunfish were exhausted. When they could no longer tell another story, it was dark. So enraptured by the stories, both the storytellers and the villagers did not realize that not only had one day passed but two.

"Aren't you hungry?" asked the headwoman of the eastern village, chuckling.

"Hearing the stories is one thing," chimed in the headwoman of the western village, "but you must not get lost in the stories. You are living and you need to eat." She began chuckling then along with her sister headwoman.

The villagers didn't find the fact that they had forgotten to eat funny. They wanted to know who won the contest. Again, they grumbled, even stomped the ground in a show of disappointment when the headwomen announced that there was still a tie.

"Can't you decide?" complained Iguana Eye.

"You two headwomen should know who won," challenged Orange Sunfish before he caught himself and said, "I mean because you are both noble and wise."

Which was when the headwomen announced in unison that there would be one more contest.

"Since you villagers now have heard all of the stories and can keep them among yourselves, both of us don't need to go away to hear and remember them for you. Therefore, each village must build a dwelling where together we can forever take turns living among you and listening to the stories. Whichever village builds the best dwelling will go to Tamalpais. Now, go home and eat and take care of yourselves and you can start in the morning."

The villagers returned the next morning, though they were none too happy.

"So, I'm wondering, since we both know the stories equally well, why representatives from both villages can't go to Tamalpais?" questioned Iguana Eye.

"And we are equally strong and brave," added Orange Sunfish. "Furthermore, my people of the western village are the finest boat builders. Our boats are well made and we are more than happy to provide our eastern neighbors a boat so that they can travel safely with us."

"And we of the eastern village, where the best chaparral grows for boat making, we will provide more chaparral to our western neighbors so that if need be they can construct more boats."

"That is all good," the headwoman of the eastern village said.

"But the contest to build the best house for my headwoman sister and me must go on," said the headwoman of the western village.

"And then truly we will see who travels the water to Tamalpais," said the headwoman of the eastern village.

Still the villagers were not at all happy. They doubted whether the headwomen would ever deem one village or the other the winner. And so both sides went to work to force the headwomen to make a decision. Unlike the stories that seemed to live in the air, a house built on the earth like none other could not be denied.

They went to work. They gathered thick branches for the walls, heavy rocks for the foundations. They were so busy that they did not notice that, after each group separated at the gorge, the headwomen could not be seen. They figured the headwomen had retreated to that secret place, wherever it was they went to converse and hear the ancient stories.

Figuring they were not being watched, they began to steal from one another, first at night, and then, after it became clear what each was doing, in broad daylight. The western villagers tore entire groves of scrub oak from the east side of the gorge. The easterners stole rocks and the best sand and dirt from the west side of the gorge. The easterners tore apart the westerners' boats for the hewed wood. Each spied the other's house, each growing taller and taller, larger and larger. They were near finished, the last stitching of roofing complete, when the headwomen, each in her own village, appeared and commanded her villagers to meet once more at the gorge.

"Now we will march west, all of us," they commanded once all of the villagers had gathered.

The westerners thought surely they had won. The eastern villagers figured that, after seeing the western house, the headwomen would go east and declare the eastern house the winner. But neither would be the case.

"Look what you have done to the eastern hills," the headwoman of the west chastened her western villagers. "The Mountain there is bare of trees. Have you forgotten the eastern village is where I come from?"

"And you," the headwoman of the eastern village said to her eastern villagers, "you have ripped rocks from the earth, leaving enormous holes. You have pulled up sand and earth along the western shore. Have you forgotten the western village is where I come from?"

Orange Sunfish, stepping forward, protested, "Well, look at this beautiful house my western villagers have created for when both of you visit us."

No sooner did he speak than Iguana Eye begin to boast about *his* villagers' giant and elaborate eastern house.

But the headwomen, raising their hands, motioned for both Iguana Eye and Orange Sunfish to stop.

"These houses are big and beautiful, but they have been built on theft and lies," began the headwoman of the eastern village. "Look," she said, pointing to the one boat left on the shore. "You have been so destructive that there is only one boat left. Both villages couldn't travel together unless one person from each village goes."

"But I don't think that was your idea when you destroyed the boats," added the headwoman of the western village, looking directly at Iguana Eye and his eastern villagers.

Iguana Eye, attempting to distract the headwoman, protested, "But you haven't even seen the big and beautiful house my villagers built for you and your sister headwoman on the other side of the gorge."

"Oh, but we have, just as we've watched you stealing from one another and destroying the land," she answered. "Have you forgotten that just as we go where we can hear the ancient stories, so too from that place can we see all that happens upon this wondrous Mountain? Have you forgotten what you yourself have said? 'Dear honorable judges, you who see the people of your villages, you who know the stories necessary to our survival, you who know and see all through the eyes of the animals and birds'? Do you remember, Iguana Eye?"

"Where is your secret place on the Mountain?" asked Orange Sunfish. "Where is it that you can hear the stories and see what we have done?"

"Anywhere there is life," the headwomen answered in unison.

"So there is no secret place?" asked Iguana Eye.

Neither headwoman bothered to answer him. Turning to the

huge house before them, they said, "The western villagers will go to this house to remember what has happened. You eastern villagers go to yours."

A long time passed, the villagers standing in silence and shame.

When the headwomen spoke again, the sun was low on the horizon, a golden hue over the open sea.

"You told the stories but didn't hear them," they said. "But don't despair. There is a winner of the contest."

The headwomen joined hands and walked to the lone boat bobbing in the water. The villagers followed. In disbelief, they watched as the two headwomen got into the boat.

"We are the winners," they proclaimed, picking up the oars.

"But you are old," said Orange Sunfish.

"What if you are attacked by the hostile villagers?" asked Iguana Eye.

"What will we do without you?" cried all the villagers.

Nodding to the large house, the headwomen said, "Tell the stories in the houses you have built. Now that you know all the stories, tell them. We may or may not return. In the meantime, we have the best story to tell whoever we meet." They pushed away from the shore and, looking back at the villagers, said, "It is what just happened, your story, the Story of the Forgetters."

Standing together, the villagers watched as the boat grew smaller and smaller, its length like the dorsal fin of a great fish, the stirring oars the flapping of birds' wings over the water.

Until Tomorrow

Question Woman, excited, exclaimed, "That's us. That's us in the story. We're in the story."

"What are you talking about?" asked Answer Woman.

"Look," said Question Woman, gesturing with her wing toward the valley. "There's the water. We're floating to Tamalpais."

Answer Woman looked to where her sister was pointing. "That's the fog, silly."

"What?"

"While I was telling the story of the storytelling contest, the fog filled the valley and came up the Mountain. Lesson number one: Pay attention to where you are. Look how dark it's gotten. We must get going."

"It's my fault," said Question Woman. "I'm sorry. I was the one begging for another story. I won't do it again."

"Until tomorrow," laughed Answer Woman.

Answer Woman lifted off the fence rail, and Question Woman did the same, both of them following the treetops above the fog, home.

Acknowledgments

Gratitude to Angela Hardin, who read and typed every word. And to my dear friends Mark and Jane Ciabattari, Susan Moore, Andrea Lerner, and Scott Lankford, who also read every word and offered encouragement along the way. Hollis Robbins, you, too, read and continued to support me so kindly at the university. Emmerich Anklam, you are the kindest and smartest of editors; what a blessing you are for a writer. And Lisa K. Marietta, my copy editor at Heyday, a genius. Speaking of Heyday, a huge shout-out for the support and for all the wonderful work you do to keep California Indigenous cultures alive. Steve Wasserman, you steer the Heyday tule boat well. And I can't forget Joan Baez for her friendship and inspiration over the years. Caryl and Mickey Hart, thank you for knowing I needed a horse, and I am thankful that, after all this time, you continue to put up with the mare's at times unpleasant alpha female behavior. And, of course,

I won't ever forget my family and people, the Federated Indians of Graton Rancheria. And then there's Jorge Leija Martinez: your heart is in each and every word here. Bendiciones, amigo.

About the Author

GREG SARRIS is currently serving his sixteenth term as Chairman of the Federated Indians of Graton Rancheria and his first term as board chair for the Smithsonian's National Museum of the American Indian. He is also a member of the Board of Regents of the University of California. His publications include *Keeping Slug Woman Alive* (1993), *Mabel McKay: Weaving the Dream* (1994, reissued 2013), *Grand Avenue* (1994, reissued 2015), *Watermelon Nights* (1998, reissued 2021), *How a Mountain Was Made* (2017, published by Heyday), and *Becoming Story* (2022, published by Heyday). Greg lives and works in Sonoma County, California. Visit his website at greg-sarris.com.